ONE LAST HEIST

DAHLIA DONOVAN

————HOT TREE PUBLISHING————

For information, contact the publisher, Hot Tree Publishing. WWW.HOTTREEPUBLISHING.COM

EDITING: HOT TREE EDITING

COVER DESIGNER: SOXSATIONAL COVER ART

FORMATTING: RMGRAPHX

PHOTOGRAPHER: FURIOUSFOTOG

ISBN: 978-1-925655-75-9

To Debbie.

ALSO BY DAHLIA DONOVAN

THE SIN BIN
THE WANDERER
THE CARETAKER
THE BOTANIST
THE ROYAL MARINE
THE UNEXPECTED SANTA
THE LION TAMER
HAKA EVER AFTER

TRADE ME
FOUND YOU

STANDALONE
AFTER THE SCRUM
THE MISGUIDED CONFESSION
ONE LAST HEIST
FORGED IN FLOOD

CHAPTER ONE

TOSHIRO

"Would you just admit you can't see in the dark?" Toshiro snapped in pure frustration. "*Mack*. Are you listening to me?"

"I'm fine. My ears work perfectly."

Fine.

He's fine.

Right.

Fine, my arse.

Well, my arse is fine.

"You walked into the table." Toshiro watched in the darkened room through the night vision on his camera while his stubborn husband stumbled around. "And into the sofa—oh, and the wall. *Classic.* You're supposed to crack the safe, not take a header into it."

"Toshi," Mack whispered his nickname sharply. "Couldn't you yell at me in Cantonese or Japanese or any one of the hundred languages you speak? It would still be distracting, but I wouldn't understand a word of it."

"I speak thirty languages—not a hundred." Toshiro grinned even though Mack couldn't see it. "I suppose the point of a timed run-through of cracking the safe might require your full attention. Oh, look, you tripped over the carpet again."

"*Toshiro Ueda-Easton.*"

"*Gregor Tempest Mackay Ueda-Easton.* Fine, fine. I'll be quiet. Continue walking into the wall, but I'm not explaining your concussion to the others." Toshiro continued to ramble about the idiotic stubbornness of his husband in Portuguese, one of the many languages he'd picked up over the years. "Idiota."

"I understood that one." Mack tossed one of the drill bits of his safe-drilling rig in his husband's general direction— missing him completely. "Keep cussing me out in Spanish."

"Portuguese."

"I swear to fucking God, Toshi." Mack dropped the drill when the timer beeped. "Damn it."

Cackling in amusement, Toshiro flipped on the lights, ignoring the continued grumbling from Mack. They'd known each other since they'd attended the same primary school in Camden in North West London. They'd fallen in love in their teens and stayed together ever since, marrying as soon as it was legally possible.

"Want another go?" Toshiro pulled his legs up to sit cross-legged on the desk in the centre of the living room of their London loft. They'd used some of their ill-gotten gains to purchase the spacious converted warehouse along the

River Thames several years ago. "Or perhaps you'd finally like to take the advice of your doctor?"

"Not now, love." Mack plopped down on top of the safe with a disgruntled groan. "I can do this."

"All right, Captain Santa," Toshiro teased him with the nickname. "Why don't we have a cup of coffee first?"

Both men had kept day jobs to hide their less-legal lives. Mack played philanthropist with his non-profit dedicated to helping feed children. They'd been the ones to gift him with the moniker of Captain Santa. It was only slightly ironic given the long history of piracy running through both sides of his family.

Mack could trace his lineage directly to the seventeenth-century British pirate. Toshiro's father also had a similarly less than illustrious family heritage delving back into piracy in the eighteenth century. They joked that in some ways, they chose to pay homage to their ancestry with their heists.

Hopping off the desk, Toshiro made his way through the open loft towards the kitchen. He put the kettle on and began getting everything together to brew the most robust coffee possible. They'd need it to get through the dry run for their next job.

"I can do this," Mack muttered, mostly to himself.

The diagnosis had come early in life for Mack when his parents noticed his sensitivity to light. They'd no idea Retinitis Pigmentosa ran in his mother's family. Aside from wearing sunglasses frequently, he'd never shown any signs of the disorder progressing further.

Until now.

Now in his thirties, Mack had slowly begun to develop problems with his night vision. He stumbled into things—struggled to drive after the sun went down. As Toshiro didn't have a license, it had been difficult for his husband to deny that particular issue, but he'd made a valiant effort at it.

A thief needs his eyesight.

It had been the argument Mack made anytime Toshiro tried to convince him to visit the doctor. As if somehow not going meant the disorder wouldn't progress. It would. Denial didn't accomplish anything aside from annoying everyone around him.

"You're brooding again." Mack wrapped his arms around Toshiro, resting his chin on his husband's shoulder. He tilted his head to smirk cheekily at him. "What've I done wrong this time?"

Glancing up at their reflection in the window, Toshiro took a moment to admire the contrasts and similarities in their appearance. They'd always made a handsome couple. Both stood tall at six foot even, with lithe, athletic bodies earned from years of being active and taking care of themselves.

While Toshiro could thank his Japanese mother for his silky ink-black hair and equally dark eyes, his British father had gifted him with a slightly lighter golden tone to his skin—one that came naturally where his husband usually required quite a bit of time outside to earn his sun-warmed appearance. Mack had wavier coal-black hair and hazel eyes that glinted mischievously.

Toshiro placed his hand flat against his husband's

gorgeous face to push him away. "Go get the sugar if you want some in your coffee."

"Bit late for a coffee." Mack dutifully wandered over to the cabinet to grab the small bowl with the sugar. "I'm rusty. Just need a bit of practise. I can do the safe."

"Rusty?" Toshiro shook his head, sending his hair into his eyes. He impatiently shoved it out of the way. "We've decades of experience between the two of us. It's not your abilities. It's your eyes."

"My eyes are perfectly fine." Mack slammed the sugar dish on the counter; a long crack almost immediately developed from the base to the rim. "Bugger."

Toshiro carefully prised his husband's clenched fingers off the ceramic container and set it to the side. "Yes, you're *perfectly* fine and handling all of this calmly and thoughtfully."

Mack spun away from him, folding his arms across his chest and staring across the loft. "I thought I had more time."

"So did I."

And he had. Though in all honesty, Mack had managed to go years beyond what the doctors had thought possible before his sight worsened. His luck had finally begun to run out.

"I can do this," Mack whispered.

Toshiro watched him with worried eyes, making a promise to himself. *And if you can't, I'll be right here to pick up the pieces for you.* "First, coffee."

"Coffee is not the answer to everything."

"Sacrilege." He grinned a bit too brightly, trying to play

into Mack's efforts at lightening the mood. "Is that a hint at you wanting decaf?"

"I'll take you over my lap and spank you if you trick me into that nasty shit again." Mack wandered out of the kitchen to where they'd set up the replica workspace for their upcoming heist. "Who even uses old-school safes anymore?"

"Let's go back to the spanking; it's far more exciting." He poured out coffee, adding sugar to one of the mugs. "We could always fob this job off entirely on Charlie and Dom, leave them to do the work while we stay here."

His twin sister, Charlie, and her partner in crime and life, Dominica Floyd, often joined them on complicated jobs. He knew the two women would have no issues pulling off a simple safecracking. One glance at the steely glare on his husband's face told him it was a waste of breath to argue the point.

"Since when do you throw work your sister's way without taking part? Besides, didn't they run off on a pretend honeymoon?" Mack grabbed his coffee and threw his arm around Toshiro's shoulder to lead him over to the floor-to-ceiling windows to stare out across their view of the River Thames. "We'll manage as a group."

Translation?

He'll stubborn his way through until it's no longer possible.

Ignoring the tightening of the hand curled around his shoulder, Toshiro leaned into his husband. Their heads rested together while they watched the movements on the river. He was glad they'd opted for the floor-to-ceiling windows with privacy film that kept anyone from seeing inside the flat.

They'd enjoyed more than a few naked moments in front of those windows. Toshiro had made sure the privacy tinting worked *before* indulging his nudist tendencies. *No accidental flaunting of my bits before the neighbours.* Mack, on the other hand, hadn't been overly bothered by strutting around before queen and country.

Not the craziest place we've had sex either.

"What are you thinking about, Mr Ueda-Easton?" Mack teased him.

"Stockholm."

Mack's grin widened even further. "Ah yes, the time you almost got me arrested because you couldn't keep the jewels in your pants."

"Me?" Toshiro elbowed him in the side. "You practically ripped my clothes off to get at *my jewels.*"

"You kept rubbing your cock against my arse while we were stuck in the closet waiting for the museum to close." Mack chuckled wickedly.

"I did not."

"Liar." Mack lifted his mug in salute. "Drink your coffee, Toshi."

"Malaka."

"Stop calling me an arsehole in Greek." Mack dodged away from him. "And don't use your pointy elbows of doom on me. I've a low tolerance for pain."

"But a high tolerance for overacting?" Toshiro held his

hand up to stop the quote he knew would be flung his way next. "I never mock anyone's pain next. You're not allowed to pick the movies we watch for a month."

"Ready for another attempt?"

He shook his head slowly, fingers still clamped around the warm mug. "Why don't we enjoy our evening?"

"We only have a few more days to prepare." Mack set his mug on the counter to head over to retrieve his tool. "Get the lights."

"Mack."

"Get the lights."

"Gregor." He wanted to address the issue, while the desperation in his husband's eyes told him Mack had no intention of discussing it. "Okay."

If he drills his hand because he can't see in the dark, I reserve the right to laugh at his stubborn arse.

And even in his head, the attempt to laugh off his worry fell completely flat.

CHAPTER TWO

MACK

"He has a point."

"*Oi*. I told you about this so you could give me advice—not so you could agree with Toshi." Mack glared at his mentor, refusing to admit defeat. Rafe Bishop had slipped into a father role, guiding him through his career when his own dad had been caught by the police and given a life sentence for his part in a series of armed robberies. "And he's not right."

Rafe leaned back in the chair, taking a casual puff from his cigar. "Maybe you should take a break, yeah? Instead of playing philanthropist to avoid suspicion, actually be one for a bit. You might enjoy it."

"How about no? Is no good?" Mack stretched his arm out to nick one of the cigars. Rafe always got the best. "I'm not surrendering to the inevitable, because that's a shitty way to live my life."

"Noble."

Mack narrowed his eyes at Rafe, wondering if he'd imagined the hint of derision in his voice. He lit his cigar and decided to stop overthinking. "I'm not tired of playing Robin Hood."

"I told your father reading you all those stories as a child would mess with your mind. What self-respecting thief has rules to steal by?" Rafe had always disapproved of Mack's approach to thievery. His mentor had wealthy tastes and chose jobs accordingly. "What great crusade are you on now?"

"There's nothing wrong with having a code to how one lives." Mack puffed strongly on the cigar while holding his lighter to it. *Damn things.* "I'm not on a crusade."

"Oh yes, the Easton Heist Rules." Rafe snorted derisively. "What was number one again?"

"Do your research."

"Well, can't argue with that one. Though you did steal it from me." Rafe had always insisted on careful observation before a single step was taken towards acquiring an object. "And two?"

"No weapons." Mack had seen first-hand the dangers of being armed. "Yes, I know you think I'm a nutter for it, but Mum died because someone got trigger happy."

Rafe waved off his argument. "Let's not revisit that unhappy history. What's the other ridiculous twaddle you insist your crew keep? Oh yes, number three, don't steal from good people. Who decides on the morality of your victims?" he demanded, then continued before Mack could answer the question. "And four, no unnecessary risks. Our entire lifestyle is an unnecessary risk."

Fair point.

"Are we revisiting your disdain for my choices for any particular reason?" Mack wouldn't have made the drive across London if he'd known this was how the talk would go. "Shall we list the rest of them to save time? Five, always have an exit strategy. Something my dad could've used to keep himself out of prison. And six, never carry your real identification. What's wrong with those?"

"How did I fail as a mentor?"

Mack sent a withering glare across the room at him. "Why am I even here?"

He'd been in the middle of proving Toshiro wrong about his ability to crack a safe in the dark when Rafe had texted him. They hadn't met up in months, not since they'd argued over a series of heists his mentor had gotten wrapped up in with an up-and-coming new face on the scene, Mary Shipton, a young woman who he'd taken under his wing. She was talented but had a tendency to run over anyone in her way.

And she just sets my sodding teeth on edge.

Something's wrong with her.

"Well?" Mack prompted after Rafe simply continued to smoke and sip from his glass of cognac. "Going to share why you summoned me?"

"I could use your expertise." Rafe held a hand up when Mack went to respond. "And the twins."

"Ahh." He rolled his eyes at the sixty-year-old who loved to draw out a tease. "Weren't you the one to tell me not to try to con a conman?"

"Good advice, that." Rafe saluted him with his crystal glass. "What would it take for you, Toshiro, and his twin sister to join me?"

"No." Mack set his cigar down, making the quick decision to leave now before they devolved into an argument like the last time. "I've heard rumours, Rafe. You're treading in dangerous waters."

"Not all of us can afford to pretend to let our better angels win, Gregor." Rafe set his drink on a nearby table and got to his feet. "If you won't help, don't push your false morality onto me."

Mack dropped his cigar into the ashtray. He couldn't help but grimace at the suddenly bitter taste in his mouth. "Why don't I see myself out?"

Stepping over to him, Rafe pulled him into a strong and intensely uncomfortable embrace. They stayed in the hug until Mack pushed his mentor away. He hated the rift that had begun to develop between them over the last year or two, but he couldn't pretend it wasn't there.

"Sure you won't join us?" Rafe shifted to the side with an arm still around Mack's shoulders to walk him towards the entrance of his impressive mansion. "You know you can trust me. I'd never steer you wrong. It could make a decent amount of money for all of us."

Mack waved off the offer with a forced smile, pushing the arm off his shoulder. "I'll think about it."

Trouble is… I don't trust you anymore, Rafe.

Not after the last time—not entirely.

Rafe followed him down the stairs to the Fiat 500 parked in the driveway. "Shouldn't you have a rule about forgiveness? I made a mistake."

"A conscious decision isn't an accident, Rafe." Mack slid into the seat of his *borrowed* Fiat. He chose to never own vehicles but borrowed a different one each month from a car dealer mate of his. "And your *mistake* cost Jude the use of his legs."

"He knew the risks." Rafe rested his hands on the roof of the vehicle, leaning down to speak through the open door. "We all—"

"Enough." Mack slammed his hand against the steering wheel. "We're having the same bloody conversation we had last time. I'm not fond of remakes. They're usually piss-poor versions of the original."

"Mind your temper. It gets you into trouble." Rafe eased away from the Fiat. "Bring Toshiro the next time you visit. I enjoy the exotic."

Mack gripped the steering wheel so tightly it creaked at the blatant prod at his husband's mixed heritage. "Don't be a racist arsehole, Bishop. You're a better man than that."

I hope.

CHAPTER THREE

"Does your husband know we're having coffee?"

Toshiro flicked a sugar cube at the hazel-eyed, blond-haired man sitting across from him. "No, because he'd handle it so well if I said I had a meeting with one of the senior detectives attached to the Interpol branch in Manchester."

"As I'm his uncle, I'm confident he'd get over it." Pierce Siddall was Mack's maternal uncle—and his only living relative not currently in prison. He'd eschewed the family business to pursue a career in law enforcement, a decision that estranged him from the majority of his kin. "How is my nephew?"

"Visiting with Bishop." Toshiro tried his best not to involve himself in the relationship between Mack and the man his husband considered his mentor. He'd never truly liked Rafe. "The first time since the accident."

"Of course, Rafe bloody Bishop." Pierce tilted his head

to stare at the ceiling for several seconds. "I'm only in London for a few days for a workshop. Do you think Mack would meet with me?"

Toshiro wanted to say yes if only to offer hope to the man who'd been without his family. He could easily see the longing in his eyes. "Maybe."

"Maybe?" Pierce chuckled wryly. "Aren't people in your line of work supposed to be better liars?"

"Travel writers?" Toshiro didn't bat an eyelash, pulling out his phone to flip through to show his uncle-in-law his latest article. "Did you read my latest?"

Part of their lifestyle involved keeping a legitimate front for their travels. Mack played the philanthropist, using the wealth amassed over the years by the Easton family to pay for it. Toshiro followed in his own father's footsteps as a writer.

It worked.

Who would suspect a well-known philanthropist and his journalist husband of being master thieves?

No one, except for Pierce, but he had an unfair advantage.

"I did. I'm also aware of a notorious painting that's been missing since the Nazi invasion of Poland suddenly reappearing in the gallery of the granddaughter of the artist." Pierce watched Toshiro for almost a minute before continuing. He seemed amused at his nephew-in-law's lack of reaction. "Interestingly, yet another piece of art of equal value from her collection has gone on the market for sale. Odd coincidence that my nephew's non-profit organisation is going to benefit from the proceeds."

"You find it odd when people donate money to charity?" Toshiro bit back a smirk when the detective choked on a sip of coffee. "Think of how the children will benefit from all the lovely millions."

"And the administration fees?"

"Merely the cost of doing good deeds." Toshiro always enjoyed playing word games with the police, particularly Pierce who knew enough of the truth to be both annoyed and amused with him. "So, why did you want to meet?"

"I can't go into details, but we're starting to investigate a series of antiquities and other items going missing from embattled cities across Syria and Iraq. Authorities initially believe…." Pierce trailed off when his phone buzzed; he checked the message then returned his attention to Toshiro. "Well, that part doesn't matter, what does is we believe there is a connection to a European-based group."

"Mack wouldn't touch war spoils—neither would I." He and his husband had strong views on the theft of cultural items. They'd spent much of their career as so-called master thieves working to return artefacts to original owners who usually offered them a decent payment out of gratitude. "Why ask me about it?"

"Rumours."

"Rumours?" Toshiro frowned at Pierce when he didn't offer anything further. "Care to share?"

"Heard young Ybarra had a cache of items for sale." Pierce nonchalantly stirred his coffee while his eyes stayed on Toshiro, likely waiting for a reaction of some sort. "Would you know about it? He's a friend of yours, isn't he?

You've both taken him under your wing."

"Nico's a good kid." Toshiro had known the transgender man since Nico was a teen. He and Mack had run into him on the job and afterwards helped him out. Now in his mid-twenties, he'd made quite a name for himself as a fence, taking stolen goods and selling them at a profit for both himself and his thief clients. "You leave him alone, Pierce Siddall."

They continued with their drinks and sandwiches. Toshiro couldn't help thinking Pierce had something else on his mind. He settled in to wait it out, not wanting to press the man.

They'd all been relatively close at one point, particularly in Mack's youth. When Pierce's career led him from homicide detective to Interpol liaison, it had brought an end to the regular visits. Toshiro could easily understand the reason; his husband hadn't wanted to put his uncle in an awkward position.

The old adage of "what you don't know can't hurt you" rang true. Despite knowing the family legacy of piracy and thievery, Pierce never once attempted to draw them out. Toshiro often worried about what might happen if a day came when their paths crossed on a job.

Would Pierce look the other way? Or would he abandon family ties to stay true to the law? Toshiro would put a healthy amount of money on the detective protecting his nephew above anything else.

Even if Mack doesn't think Pierce is capable of it.

"Toshiro?"

He shook his head to clear it of the worry that had clouded his thoughts. "Sorry. Did I miss something?"

Pierce appeared to pause to consider his words before continuing. "Nothing important. Just be careful—the both of you. I've never wanted to know what you're into but this investigation I'm part of might lead somewhere catastrophic."

Right.

Well, that's comforting, isn't it?

"We're always careful." Toshiro smiled through the concern gnawing in his belly. His instincts told him to heed the warning. "So, Mr Detective Inspector, are you paying or am I?"

CHAPTER FOUR

MACK

His meeting with Rafe had left him unsettled, and returning to an empty loft hadn't improved his mood. He found a Post-it Note on a packet of leftovers in the fridge. *Out for lunch. Eat something other than beans on toast. Love, T.* Rolling his eyes at his husband's teasing, he grabbed the curry from the previous night and heated it up.

Setting it on the coffee table in the living room, Mack dragged the table closer to the sofa. He perused floor plans of a villa in Italy near Positano. Once owned by an arms dealer, it had been turned into a rental property for anyone who could afford the exorbitant rates.

Rumours circulated of a hidden treasure hidden underneath one of the tiled mosaic floors. Mack always believed in relieving merchants of death of their spoils of war. He didn't know what they might find, but they'd either fence the stolen items or return them to their rightful owners.

He made a mental note to check in with his crew to

ensure they were prepared. Nico already had a few buyers in mind for whatever they found. The kid had proved to be gifted at moving stolen goods.

Can't really call him a kid at twenty-six.

Makes me sound like a grumpy old man.

The security system beeped signalling Toshiro's arrival just as he finalised their plans. His husband trudged across the living room, threw himself onto the couch, and rested his head in Mack's lap. He grinned winningly up at Mack until he moved the papers out of his way.

"It's barely three in the afternoon. How are you exhausted?" Mack stretched his arm across his husband to gather up the documents on the coffee table. He playfully bumped Toshiro on the nose with his elbow. "What exactly were you doing for lunch?"

"Eating food."

"Prat." He flicked his husband on the forehead. "Ready for our Italian adventure?"

"Sure. Can I have a preview of the salami?" Toshiro snickered before flipping around on his stomach and propping himself up on his elbows. "Well? Pop it out for me? I'm waiting. Serve me my meat."

"You're a prat."

"Am I a prat who's getting his sausage?" Toshiro gave an exaggerated lick of his lips, which only made Mack laugh even harder. "I'm dangerously close to your meat stick, and you're snickering at me."

"You're attempting to deflect me away from your supper." Mack had to admit, as his husband shifted up further to balance on one arm while his other hand deftly undid the button and zipper on his jeans, the distraction definitely worked. "Who am I to deny a starving man his supper?"

The dark eyes that had been full of amusement moments before now glittered with desire. Mack shuffled down on the couch to provide easier access, lifting his hips up to allow Toshiro to shove down his jeans and boxers. His fingers slid through the silky strands of hair brushing against his thighs; he always enjoyed it when his husband grew out his hair.

"I've missed you." Toshiro directed his comment to Mack's cock, much to his amusement; his husband's lips curved up into a wickedly teasing smile. "Thank heavens I'm not a vegetarian."

"No, but you are a—" Mack almost bit the tip of his tongue when Toshiro engulfed his hardening shaft completely. "Damn it, Toshi."

All thoughts of heists, secretive lunch dates, and teasing comments flew out of his mind. Mack's entire world narrowed to the mouth hungrily devouring his erection. Toshiro slipped his hand between his thighs, which Mack spread to allow better access.

Leaning his head up slightly, Toshiro made a show of sucking on two of his fingers before lowering down again on Mack's shaft. His hand delved deeper between his husband's thighs until he found his target. The slick digits teased Mack before dipping inside with relative ease.

"Bugger," Mack grunted. He started to slowly undulate between Toshiro's mouth and fingers. "Fuck. I love your tongue."

Toshiro tugged on a hair on his thigh. "And?"

Mack smirked at him and pushed his head back down to continue. "Yes, I love more than your tongue, but it's right at the top of the list at the moment."

The almost casual licking and sucking grew into a more fevered pace. Mack bucked up into his husband's warm mouth, then back against the now three fingers pressing into him. It was brilliantly perfect and yet not enough at the same time.

He craved more.

Always.

"Problem?" Toshiro asked when Mack gently lifted his head up using his hold on his hair. "Gregor?"

"Fuck me," Mack hissed when Toshiro continued to piston his fingers into him. "*Toshi.*"

The confusion evaporated from his husband's face immediately. Toshiro gracefully rolled off the couch onto his feet. He grabbed Mack by the arm to drag him towards the windows.

"Easy there." Mack tripped over his jeans when they slipped down to his ankles. He kicked off his trainers, and then his trousers and boxers. "If I take a header out the window, you'll have a lot of explaining to do."

Leaning against one of the panes of the floor-to-ceiling windows, Mack lazily stroked his cock while watching Toshiro undress. He never tired of the slow reveal of his husband's beautifully golden skin. His eyes traced over the supple muscles, the barbell piercings through his nipples, and the intricately inked Japanese-style Phoenix tattoo covering his entire left arm from shoulder to wrist.

Fuck.

He's beautiful.

Why the hell did he marry me again?

Toshiro slid a hand up his own chest, toying with one of the barbells. "Avoir le feu au cul."

"Did you just say my arse was on fire?" Mack blinked at Toshiro.

"Some phrases shouldn't be directly translated; you lose a bit of the meaning." He grinned at him; his fingers still toying with his piercing.

"I'll assume it meant something sexually enthralling as you certainly sounded sexy as fuck when you said it." Mack closed the distance between them and swung Toshiro around to press him against the window. Their lips connected in a bruising kiss that left him breathing in hard gasps. "You're so bloody gorgeous. Why'd you marry an old pirate like me?"

"First, we're the same age." Toshiro lunged forward to bite Mack's bottom lip, sucking on it before easing away. "Second, you're hung like a horse. Why wouldn't I marry you?"

"Prat." Mack snaked a hand around to swat his husband on the arse. "Thought you wanted my money?"

"That too," he teased. "Up against the wall and spread 'em. Time to play fruit monger and thoroughly inspect the merchandise."

They shared several bruising kisses until a breathless Toshiro shoved him back. He dropped to his knees. His mouth easily found Mack's cock again.

After another demonstration of his skilfully agile tongue, Toshiro got to his feet, and Mack found himself pressed against the glass. He groaned loudly when his husband nudged between his cheeks before sinking his shaft into him. *God, I love him.*

With one hand planted firmly against the window, Mack reached around to catch his husband by the neck. He stretched his neck to the right, allowing for a slightly awkward kiss. Their mouths separated as Toshiro picked up his pace.

He leaned forward with his forehead bumping against the glass lightly. "Stroke me," Mack ordered desperately. "Damn it, Toshi."

Pushing up into him harder, Toshiro looped his arm around to run his fingers across Mack's lower abdomen before drifting further down. Between the seesawing shaft inside him and the hand on his own erection, he didn't need long to crest the edge of orgasm. He locked his knees to keep from hitting the floor and taking his husband with him.

A few seconds later, Toshiro drove into him one last time before exploding with his own pleasure. Mack panted rapidly before eventually twisting around to wrap his arms around his husband tightly. They barely managed to stay on their feet.

Mack gingerly inched them both towards the nearby bathroom. They cleaned up and returned to collapse on the couch, still naked. "Was the sausage to your liking?"

"Oh my God. Put your clothes on."

Mack burst out laughing when Toshiro grabbed cushions

from the couch to cover both of their crotches. They'd apparently missed the sound of Charlie Ueda, his husband's twin sister, entering the loft. "Cover your eyes."

"They are covered," she shouted, her hands strategically placed over her face. "I'm so going to have nightmares about this."

"Don't be a drama queen." Toshiro hopped off the couch to collect their randomly discarded clothing. He tossed Mack's jeans and boxers over to him before turning to address his sister. "What have I told you about knocking?"

"Why give me the code and a key if I'm not supposed to enter? Besides, it's the middle of the afternoon. I assumed you'd be fully clothed." She bumped into the wall attempting to walk with her eyes closed and covered with her hands. "Dom dropped me off since she's got to do the shopping."

"We're decent." Mack finished zipping up his trousers, propping his bare feet on the coffee table to relax on the couch.

"You're covered," she retorted tartly. "Not necessarily decent."

"Lesbians who get caught naked in glass houses shouldn't throw morality stones." Mack saluted her when she flipped him off. "Am I wrong?"

They'd teased Charlie and Dominica mercilessly when they'd been busted in a greenhouse having a moment to themselves. The two women had lost track of time when the twins' mother stumbled onto them. Mack wasn't sure who'd been more traumatised by it.

"Is it a hug or a no hug day?" Toshiro sat on the arm of

the couch to pull on his socks and shoes.

"It's a no hug day." Charlie slipped her hand into the pocket of her hoodie where Mack knew she always kept a squishy ball to help her stim. "Maybe tomorrow. Mum wants to know when we'll be back from Italy."

"Five days—a week max." Mack rifled through the papers nearby to wave the jotted-down itinerary at her. "Are you still coming with us?"

As an autistic, Charlie had days when the world simply overwhelmed her. They'd learned how to work around her quirks and limits. She wouldn't be herself without them.

When they were kids, the fraternal twins had fought many battles in school. Toshiro had always stood by her side—not in front of her. They'd gotten into a fair few fights as a result.

"I'm mentally prepared for it. Got my headphones. Got my Rubix cube. Got my Dommy." Charlie wandered into the kitchen. "And I don't mean that in the BDSM way, you perverts. Tempy, do you still have Weetabix?"

"In your cabinet." Mack chose to ignore her favourite nickname for him. She insisted if his parents wanted to call him Tempest, it was a crime not to use the name, or at least a variation of it. "We even got a new box just for you."

Charlie returned several minutes later with a large bowl of Weetabix, yoghurt, strawberries, and honey. She clutched it possessively in her arms while Mack grimaced at the mixture. "Did you pick our seats on the plane yet?"

Toshiro nicked one of her strawberries on his way past before collapsing on the couch next to Mack. "First class, window seat, and we bought out the seats behind so you don't have to stress about someone behind you."

"Is your Dommy stopping by for supper?" Mack asked. As neither of the twins had a license, he and Charlie's girlfriend found themselves playing chauffeur quite a bit. "Or are you braving public transport?"

Charlie jabbed her spoon repeatedly into the breakfast cereal. "Do you mind if we have supper here?"

"Have we ever minded?" Toshiro stretched his arm across Mack, waving his fingers to demand another berry. She frowned at him but finally offered the bowl to him. "Want to make baked *katsudon* with me? You make a better broth than me."

"Fine." She shrugged.

"Just fine?" he prompted.

And silence. Charlie twisted around in her chair to face away from them. She focused her entire attention on her snack. Mack glanced over at his husband, who watched his fraternal twin in concern.

Mack drew Toshiro's attention to his plans since Charlie clearly needed time to process something. He grabbed the tablet underneath the floor plans. "Check out these emails Jude managed to get from our merchant of death about the villa."

"How do we know he hasn't been back since to retrieve all of it?" Toshiro scrolled the emails with him. "I would've done."

"Right. Imagine you've got stolen goods, some gold, and cash hidden in a villa. What better place to keep it hidden than in a home you've sold? Jude found the contract of the sale. It's gone to a business he owns. So technically, he's laundered millions of stolen funds through real estate. Not only that, but he's managed to make a fortune renting out the place." Mack had to admire the genius method of shuffling around funds. He might have to use the scam to deal with his own earnings. "He's essentially maintained complete control of any and all construction done."

"Cagy bastard."

And he was.

"Clever and cagy," Mack agreed readily. "Given he's dug underneath a villa, created an underground safe, and had a forger recreate the appearance of the mosaic tiles."

And we'll have to be even cleverer to steal it all out from under him without him having a clue.

Piece of cake.

CHAPTER FIVE

TOSHIRO

"Honey, I'm home." Dom had first knocked, then used her code to get into the loft. "I come bearing gifts."

The only American in their crew, Dom had grown up in England. Both of her parents had worked as diplomats after long careers in the Air Force. She'd spent most of her youth learning how to mingle amongst politicians and the upper crust of society.

A gifted artist, Dom had studied art at the University College London. She worked as an art restorer as a front. Her skills lay in creating all manner of forgeries, from documents to paintings.

She'd met Charlie at university and had been intrigued by the quiet mouse who hid behind a book in the corner during every class. Toshiro had been awed by how much the African-American woman had brought his twin out of her shell. She didn't baby or patronise his sister as many others tended to do.

"You're thinking some lofty thoughts, T-man." Dom blew a kiss at Charlie and joined him in the kitchen. "You might break something."

"If you want supper, you'll behave yourself." He waved a spatula at her.

"What's on your mind?" She always had a sixth sense about people around her. They'd learned to trust her instincts when it came to human nature. "Well?"

"Do they not teach patience in America?"

"I've spent a grand total of five years of my life in the States—and they weren't even consecutive. Don't think you'll distract me like you do your boy toy."

"Boy toy?" Toshiro laughed so hard that he had to grip the edge of the counter. "I'll give you twenty quid to say it when Mack can hear you."

"Done deal." She grabbed one of the nearby chairs, spun it around to sit on it backwards. "Well?"

"He met with Bishop again." Toshiro couldn't quite get the older man out of his mind. Rafe tended to keep secrets and use people. He worried Mack would be blinded by his attachment to the man. "I can't shake the feeling something isn't quite right with him."

"Aside from his being a shady dickhead?"

"Yes." He peered across the room to see Mack fully involved on his laptop, then shifted closer to Dom, lowering his voice. "Met with Pierce Siddall. You know, Mack's uncle?"

"The cop?"

"That's the one." Toshiro paused to check on the onions

in the pan. He didn't get to finish his thought when Charlie joined them. "It's not quite ready yet."

The conversation would clearly wait for another day. Charlie stepped up to help him slice up the fully rested breaded pork. They added it to the onions along with the sauce, stock, and whisked egg; his mouth already watering for the *katsudon*.

"Could one of you check on the rice?" Toshiro asked.

While Dom got the rice out of the cooker, Charlie clambered onto the counter to reach the bowls on the top shelf of the cabinet. His sister had inherited the typical Ueda height, or lack of it, standing at barely five foot two. He'd gotten his six feet from his father's side of the family.

"Here's to the last supper before we leave for Naples." Dom saluted them all once they'd sat down to eat. "Cheers."

Let's hope it all goes easy-peasy.

They'd barely gotten halfway through dinner when a ring on his phone drew Toshiro away from the table. He grabbed his mobile to check the message. *Bishop?* The man never reached out to him; they got on like oil and water.

Rafe: Would you ask your sister to respond to my email? I've a job that requires her delicate touch.

Toshiro: No.

Rafe: Don't be petulant. It's a zero risk task.

Toshiro: No.

Rafe: Must you be such a child?

Toshiro: I'd rather lick the toilets clean at Wembley stadium than continue this conversation.

Sodding bastard.

Toshiro blocked the number to prevent another text from Rafe. *Right. Deal with the job in Italy first, then I can find a way to deal with Bishop without Mack getting hacked off at me.*

* * *

Spread out across three separate flights, their crew made the trip from London to Naples with no issues. They connected after their respective planes landed to make the less than two-hour drive along the coast together. Toshiro made sure the group took at least a brief moment to enjoy the beautiful Amalfi Coast before getting to work.

Given the nature of the area with its steep hills and plethora of stairs and narrow walkways, Jude had opted to remain at home. He could easily offer his technical support from a distance. Toshiro had no doubts it chafed a bit to be left at home.

A problem for another day.

They'd all avoided talking about it. Toshiro, given his dislike of Rafe, hadn't been on the job in question. He knew from his sister's recounting of it that the accident had been entirely avoidable.

If Rafe hadn't been in charge.

Why is it always him?

"Toshi?"

He drew his attention away from the gorgeous Amalfi Coast and his thoughts to find Mack watching him. "Are we there yet?"

His husband chuckled quietly, but his eyes still held a

hint of concern. "You've got the same look you had that time you almost failed your maths exam."

"Thinking about Jude." Toshiro went with a half-truth, deciding to leave out the Rafe bit. "We should go check on him when we get back."

"You sure? He seems fine," Mack remarked casually. He guided the vehicle through the narrow streets of the town towards the villa. "I'll take your word for it."

He loved his husband. He really did, even if Mack occasionally failed to see things right in front of him when it came to friends and family. *Never on a job, though.*

Yet.

CHAPTER SIX

MACK

The first full day in the villa had been spent investigating. First, they made sure no security cameras or other monitoring equipment existed inside. They used an imaging device attached to a smartphone Jude got for them. It was devised to detect studs, pipes, and rodent problems.

And safes, apparently.

No matter how prepared Mack felt, there was always an element of risk to their chosen profession. The villa proved to be no different. The imaging device showed no safe lay underneath the mosaic tiles as they'd been told.

"Well, it's either deeper than four inches, which is distinctly possible, or we're wrong." Dom sat on the edge of the indoor pool with her feet dangling in the water. "Are we wrong?"

"I'm scanning every single wall." Charlie poked her head around one of the pillars with her mobile pressed against the other side. "I texted Jude. He's looking into other options since we quite obviously can't destroy every floor in the villa."

"We could." Dom flicked water at her girlfriend.

"Might make it a bit obvious." Mack lay on his back on the marble floor by the pool. He stared up at the arched ceiling to consider their options. "Well, at the very least, it'll be a lovely vacation."

While Charlie and Toshiro wandered around the house thoroughly scanning every flat surface, Mack studied through every piece of information gathered. He ignored the quietly arguing twins and Dom's splashing around. It reminded him of something his father once told him. *The prize isn't always guaranteed, Gregor. Expect to lose more often than not.*

Investigating every inch of the four-story eighteenth-century villa would take a while. Mack had booked out the place for several weeks, though they only intended to stay for one. He was reviewing the layout of each floor when it struck him.

If I were an utterly evil wanker wanting to hide my ill-gotten gains, where would I put them?

The Catholic chapel.

That's where.

"Toshi." He shot to his feet, heading by Dom and pausing to shove her into the pool. "Enjoy your swim."

"Dickhead."

"I am in possession of both a dick and a head." Mack continued through the house to find his husband on the fourth floor inspecting one of the rooms in the penthouse.

"Have you scanned the chapel yet?"

Toshiro thought about it for a second and then his eyes lit up. "Brilliant idea."

They tumbled down one staircase after another until they reached the first level. Toshi started with the floor, continuing to the walls. Mack left him to it and moved over to inspect the intricate carving above what was apparently a place to pray to the right of the altar.

His curiosity got the better of him as he ran his fingers along the inside of the alcove behind the crucifix. He noticed a notch at the base. *Interesting.* Pressing against it, he grinned when a panel to his left slid open.

"Found something."

Toshiro lifted his head up from behind a podium. "Something useful?"

"I hope so." Mack believed the payoff might be worth it, but wasn't looking forward to ripping up tiles and attempting to replace them. He reached an arm into the cavity revealed in the wall. "It's not a safe."

Pressing further into the wall, Mack eventually hooked the stack of papers hidden inside. He sat on one of the benchs and Toshiro quickly joined him. *What the bloody hell is all this?* The documents appeared to be contracts of some sort but written in a language he didn't understand.

"You're the modern language expert." Mack shoved them into Toshiro's hands. "Is it useful?"

"It's an Eastern European language, but not one I speak. Slovakian, I think." Toshiro leafed through the documents. He eased one out of the bunch. "Romanian. A couple of these are in Russian."

If Mack had to guess, the documents were not from the last year or two. They seemed aged but not antique. Not what they were looking for, but interesting enough to get a translation done.

"Take them or scan them?" Mack continued to flip through them. "Scan, I think. Not sure keeping the originals would actually do anything."

"We've got a few days. I'll send a scan to a mate of mine who does read several of the Slavic languages. She can tell us what they say." Toshiro grabbed the stack and started taking photos of them. "Anything else in your cubbyhole?"

"Sadly, not. I'm encouraged to know there are hidden spaces in the villa." Mack dragged his fingers roughly through his distracted husband's hair, using it to drag him over for a kiss. "Leave it open for now."

With Toshiro lost in language, Mack returned to thoroughly inspecting the altar and chapel. His instincts told him the secret panel was original to the villa. He doubted a man as savvy as their mark would risk using it on the off-chance a previous owner or local Italian might know about it.

An eighteenth-century villa would've seen hundreds or thousands of guests over the years. If their merchant of death had created a hidden space, it had to be in an entirely unlikely place. It was one reason why he'd believed the story of a safe under the tiles.

"Tempy?"

"Must you use that as well? I don't feel nearly as obligated to allow you to as I do with Charlie." He glanced over his shoulder to find Dom at the chapel door. His teasing fell away at the confused expression on her face. "Problem?"

"Charlie found something strange."

"Define strange." Toshiro held the phone away from his ear with obvious concern for his twin. "Good or bad?"

"Strange. Obvs." She rolled her eyes at both of them. "Are you going to come with me to see or pray for forgiveness for your many sins?"

They found Charlie sitting on the bed of one of the third-floor bedrooms. She hopped off the mattress when they entered. Mack immediately noticed one of the bookcases had been pulled slightly away from the wall.

"Found a weird line on the image that disappeared behind the bookcase. Dom and I pulled it out." Charlie caught the edge of Mack's sleeve to push him closer. "See?"

Mack eased up next to the wall to get a look. "See what you mean by weird."

"Want a light?" Toshiro pressed up behind him, holding his phone up to shine the light into the dark shadow cast by the bookcase. "This just got a bit easier—and harder."

Truer words had never been spoken. Mack could easily see the slightly raised space on the wall, definitely a new addition to the villa. Their job had gone from removing and replacing tiles to plaster instead.

It would definitely be easier than doing antique mosaic tiles, but they didn't have the supplies for plastering and painting. They couldn't head out to the shop and purchase them, either.

"Send a quick text to Jude. Get him to send a shipment to us overnight." Mack quickly made a note of what they'd need. "Dom? You're the artsy one. What sort of colour is this paint?"

"An Italian one." She grinned cheekily at him.

"Taking a hundred quid for every shit joke." Mack nudged Toshiro when he laughed. "Help me shift this thing."

Shifting the bookcase turned out to be more difficult than anticipated. Made entirely of hardwood, it weighed a ton. All four of them managed to get it out of the way without damaging the antique or themselves.

Or anything in the bloody thing.

Charlie and Dom collapsed onto the bed with an exhausted groan. Mack ignored them and his overly dramatic husband who pretended to flail on the floor. He focused his attention on deciding how best to get into whatever was hidden beneath the wall.

Using his phone, Mack photographed it from every angle with and without the flash. Ripping things up wouldn't be the problem. He was more concerned about repairing it once they were done.

The goal being to ensure no one realised anything had changed. Their mark hadn't visited the villa in years from what they'd been able to determine. Mack hoped by leaving things identical to when they arrived, would prevent any suspicions about their visit.

Speaking of which.

"Who's going sightseeing this afternoon?" Mack glanced over his shoulder to find Toshiro engaged in a fierce thumb-wrestling battle with his sister while Dom watched. "*Honestly.* Who is playing tourist so no one thinks we're doing something we shouldn't?"

"We're going to the Morelli museum." Dom grabbed Charlie by the hand to drag her off the bed. "Enjoy playing construction workers."

Mack blinked at the two women who disappeared so quickly that he wondered if they'd broken the sound barrier. "Typical. Leave us with all the hard work."

"On the plus side." Toshiro smiled wickedly at him from the floor. "We've an Italian villa completely to ourselves for hours. Heated indoor pool. Sauna. Outdoor Jacuzzi."

CHAPTER SEVEN

TOSHIRO

"Naked Jac—" Toshiro stopped abruptly when he realised Mack hadn't heard a word. His husband sat on the edge of the Jacuzzi with his gaze fixed on the beautiful view of the coastline. *Merde.* "What's going on in that handsome but thick head of yours?"

"Knobhead."

"I'd like to knob your head."

"What does that even mean?" Mack managed a forced chuckle that did nothing to allay Toshiro's concerns. "Knob my head?"

"Sure we can come up with a perverted meaning for it if we try hard enough." Toshiro waited patiently to see if his husband would confide in him. He'd been waiting for months for the other shoe to finally drop and Mack to stop brooding. "What's going on, Gregor?"

Mack patted wood beside him. "Take a seat."

Toshiro joined him on the rim of the Jacuzzi. He reached

a hand down to test the water. "It's lovely and warm."

"What if I go completely blind?"

He froze with his hand still dipped in the bubbling water. *Ahh. Okay, be confident and comforting.* "Well, you'd look good with a cane."

Right, not ideal.

Idiota.

Mack shoved him backwards into the water, fully clothed. "I'm serious. What if I go to the doctor and she says it's progressing faster and faster?"

He dragged himself towards the side to lean his arms against it. "Not seeing the doctor won't change the results, *moosh bekhoradet.*"

The Persian term of endearment made Mack laugh, as Toshiro knew it would. He'd taken to using it when learning the language. It translated to "may a mouse eat you," which made no sense in English and never failed to amuse him.

"I still say you made that shit up." Mack undressed quickly, leaving a pile of clothes on the ground, to slide into the water next to his husband. "How is a mouse eating you an admission of love?"

"Just is." He shrugged. "Being night blind or even legally blind doesn't mean your sight will be completely gone. Even if it is, we'll make it work. You're still you—stumbling into the wall or not."

"Am I still me without the heists and adventures?"

"Why did your dad read all those Robin Hood and pirate stories to you?" Toshiro reached into the water to pull off his waterlogged trainers and socks. His jeans, boxers, and shirt quickly followed. "One step at a time, Gregor. We can't avoid the doctor forever. If we know what's going on, we can deal with it."

Mack gripped him by the sides to drag him over until their bodies pressed flush against one another. "Why don't we talk about it after we get back home?"

"Procrastination, thy name is Mack." Toshiro flicked water into his husband's face. "Shouldn't we make an attempt at getting into whatever is behind the bookcase?"

"And waste being naked in a Jacuzzi under the Tuscan sun?"

"We're not actually in Tuscany," Toshiro pointed out helpfully.

"Close enough."

"Not sure the Tuscans would agree." He groaned when Mack rubbed their already hardening cocks together. "*Gregor.*"

"A little fun before we do manual labour." His husband tightened his hold on his sides, guiding him closer. "Sword fighting took on a whole new meaning after our first kiss."

Reaching up to tweak his husband's nipple, a punishment for the idiotic joke, Toshiro enjoyed the pleasurable way Mack then bucked against him. The water aided their shafts in slipping against one another. He couldn't really complain; they'd always had an unfortunate tendency to mess around with each other on the job.

The thrill of it all, maybe?

His mobile beeped from where it sat on the ground outside of the Jacuzzi. Toshiro ignored it until the emergency tone went off, one selected by his twin. He shot away from Mack, clambering out of the water to grab the iPhone.

Dom: Stop fucking in the Jacuzzi.

"Think my sister would mind if we accidentally on purpose lost Dominica in a catacomb?" He set his phone down on a nearby table. "They know us too well."

"Probably because you always forget to lock the door."

"You're an exhibitionist," Toshiro retorted. "Grab my clothes for me? I should hang them up, so they have time to dry off."

Mack ducked down under the water and came up a second later with a handful of damp fabric. He draped it over the edge of the Jacuzzi. "Sure you don't want to hop back in?"

"Work first. Play later." Toshiro decided to leave his clothes to dry where they were. He didn't trust himself not to join his husband in the water. "Get dressed."

"If you insist." Mack slowly climbed out of the water. He ran his fingers through his damp hair. "Grab one of the towels from the chest over there?"

He completely ignored his husband. *Well, not entirely, his cock has my full attention. God, he's beautiful.* "You're supposed to be getting dressed."

"Pulled a muscle in my back. Can't reach my jeans. Want to get them for me?" Mack smirked at him. He kicked at his trousers that rested on the ground at his feet. "Didn't we vow to always be there for one another?"

Sternly telling himself to keep his mind on task, Toshiro failed almost immediately. He could never resist the mischievous glint in Mack's eyes. It had been the first thing to cause him to fall in love so many years ago.

Toshiro crossed the short distance between them, stopping when they once again pressed up against one another. "What did you say about sword fighting?"

The teasing grin on Mack's face blossomed into the full-blown smile that always made Toshiro's heart skip a beat. His husband went from devilish pirate to dashing rogue in an instant. *I've really got to stop reading all those romances Charlie buys.*

Placing his hand on Mack's chest, Toshiro ran his fingers across the tattoo decorating the entire right side of his husband's body. It started at the top of his shoulders with an antique map and compass, continuing down his chest and rib cage with a pirate ship and skull. His pirate heritage fully celebrated with his body as the canvas.

"Want to walk the plank?" Mack teased when Toshiro traced the pirate ship on his left arm. "I can draw an X to mark the spot for you."

"Or a T?" Toshiro rolled his hips causing their cocks to knock into each other. "Or maybe it's an O?"

"Or is it just a new low in our terrible attempts at humour?" Mack's shoulders shook with laughter. His arms wound around Toshiro tightly. "We'd make terrible comedians."

"You laughed." He squeezed an arm between their bodies to wrap around both of their shafts. "It's why I married you."

"My cock?"

"No, you laugh at my jokes." Toshiro stroked their erections. He enjoyed watching the pleasure drift across

Mack's face. His husband's eyes had always been expressive. "Don't let me fall."

"Only if it's funny."

Leaning forward to bite Mack on the chest for the tease, Toshiro grunted when his husband brought his hand up to hold him there. He ran his tongue around the hardened nipple near his mouth. If anyone happened to be watching, he hoped they enjoyed the show.

They managed to walk carefully towards the nearby lounger still connected to each other. Mack lay down on it, drawing Toshiro down with him. They twisted around until they'd squashed together on their sides.

Perfect.

A creaking noise was the only warning before the wicker bench gave way underneath their combined weight.

Or, not so perfect.

Toshiro extracted himself from the broken wood, carefully avoiding splinters in any sensitive spots. He caught Mack's hand to help him to his feet. "This is what happens when you drink protein shakes."

"This is all muscle." Mack flicked Toshiro's nipple ring. "How do we explain the bench?"

"We don't." He picked up the pieces of it to dump over the side of the cliff. "Who's going to know?"

"Ever wanted to screw in church?"

Grabbing his husband by the hand, Toshiro led him along the path down the steps to the chapel. They'd cross one thing off their sex bucket list then return to the job at hand. What could it hurt?

Nothing.

Unless we're struck by lightning.

Dear God, who I don't necessarily believe in, please don't smite us.

CHAPTER EIGHT

MACK

The benches in the chapel were as uncomfortable as any other church bench. More so, given their age. Mack stretched out on his back, wholly sated from the pleasure of having his husband. His head rested in Toshiro's lap, who'd decided to sit and reflect.

He heard a snore.

Or take a nap.

Tilting his head faintly, Mack watched the peacefulness on his husband's face. They needed to get going soon. He waited for a few more minutes until a cramp started in his calf.

Shit.

Mack shot to his feet and reached down to carefully massage his leg. "Don't say it."

"Isn't cramping a sign of ageing?"

He tugged on one of Toshiro's piercings. "Let's find our clothes, get cleaned up, and attempt to see if we can find the safe."

They chased each other through the villa after retrieving their clothes. Toshiro draped his across the towel rack in their bathroom. They quickly dressed, only barely managing to avoid another romp in the bed.

By the time Dom and Charlie returned, the two men had managed to make a decent amount of headway in removing a section of the wall. They discovered a brilliantly concealed cavity hidden by a board that had been plastered and painted to match the rest of the room. Beneath all of it, a safe greeted them.

"Now the hard part." Toshiro dug through their gear to hand Mack his drill.

With careful precision, Mack made four small holes in the door of the safe. He took the fibre optic cable Charlie held out to him. He slid it into the first one, taking a look through the attached screen to see if it provided a view of the inside locking mechanism.

Not door number one.

Easing the cable out, Mack slipped it into the second hole. *No dice.* The third proved to be closer, but not enough. He lucked out with the last one. *Thank the goddess of piracy.*

"Tosh? Give us a hand." Mack handed over his phone that was connected to the cable. His husband held it up for him to see the screen clearly. "Right. Here I go."

"Don't bugger it up, Tempy." Dom gave him a thumbs up while Charlie shushed her girlfriend. "What? I'm helping."

Tuning the two women out, Mack started to slowly turn the dial while watching the gears within the safe's locking mechanism turn. The others remained quiet, allowing him to focus entirely on not screwing up their easiest option of getting inside. He managed it, after a carefully checking each bit lined up correctly.

He received a round of applause when the door swung open finally. "Let's see what we've got."

On first inspection, they appeared to have not much at all. Mack reached first for what seemed to be a cardboard box. He lifted it only to almost drop it in surprise at the weight of the package.

Mack shoved the lid off the box and stared in astonishment at the stacks of what he thought were 500oz gold bars. "Well, think he'll miss these?"

Toshiro reached inside to grab one, twisting it around. "No markings."

"Privately melted down and poured?" Dom took one as well and inspected it with Charlie. "These weren't bought at any bank. So, where does an arms dealer get millions of dollars' worth of gold?"

"Not sure we want to know the answer." Mack set the weighted container down on the nearby bed to return his attention to the other contents. He had a distinct feeling the gold came from stolen treasures, melted down to prevent being recognised. "*Fuck.*"

"Gregor?" Toshiro rejoined him by the safe. "What did you find?"

Mack carefully lifted out a diamond-encrusted tiara. "Didn't we confirm our mark hadn't been here for at least a year?"

"Yes," Charlie piped up from where she'd been packing away some of their equipment. "Your contact verified it for us."

Shit.

Rafe.

Tosh's going to kill me.

"Isn't that one of the jewels stolen from a museum a few months ago?" Dom poked her head between their shoulders to get a better look at it. "Belonged to some grand duchess. It's worth like a million and a half."

"Mack."

He set the tiara down and returned to the safe. "Let's see what else is in here."

"Gregor."

"Right. So, Charlie and I are going to enjoy the sauna." Dom grabbed her girlfriend by the hand and dragged her out of the room.

"Subtle." Mack rifled through the papers that had been underneath the box of gold. "I can feel you boring a hole in my head."

"Who exactly was your trusted source on this?" Toshiro asked. He reached by Mack to pick up a small box, opening it to reveal a gold coin. "Another antiquity. Why do I get the feeling Rafe Bishop's name is about to make its way into the conversation?"

"Tosh."

"Don't be cute. Don't flash those puppy-dog hazel eyes at me." Toshiro glared when Mack turned his saddest face towards him. "You're an arse."

His husband cursed him out in a few languages. Mack waited patiently for him to vent his frustration. Toshiro eventually wound down, though he continued to scowl at him.

"Let's clear this out and get it cleaned up. We can chat—in English—about how I buggered it up once we're safely home. I'd prefer not to linger now that we know he visits the villa." Mack took anything of potential from the safe, including a stack of papers, and slowly closed the door. "Am I sleeping on the couch?"

Silence.

That's a yes.

Bugger.

CHAPTER NINE

MACK

The flight home was quiet. Charlie, as always, decided he'd wronged her brother. She had pointedly ignored him for the rest of the trip, which her girlfriend found highly amusing. He'd find it funny if Toshiro hadn't given him the silent treatment as well.

Everything in Italy had gone smoothly—all things considered. They'd plastered then painted the wall, thanks to Dom's expertise, gotten it perfect, and once it was dry the bookcase had been put back in place. Until someone actually attempted to get to the safe, no one would be any the wiser.

They'd decided to use Nico to sell the gold. It split multiple ways far more simply than a tiara or the documents they'd found. The stolen jewels would be returned to their previous owner, eventually.

After two nights on the couch, Mack decided to make his way over to Jude's place. His oldest friend usually had good advice for him. *Except for that one time the night before he got married and the one time in the Netherlands.* They'd promised never to mention the time they got arrested in Amsterdam for misbehaving after accidentally on purpose eating brownies with a fun additive.

"Tired of kipping on the sofa?" Jude guided his state-of-the-art wheelchair across his living room after opening the door. "Or have you swanned over to my side of the river for some other reason?"

"Don't mock my pain."

"Okay, princess." Jude grabbed two beers, throwing one over to him. "Right. You buggered it. What do you want me to do about it?"

"Mocking my pain again." Mack collapsed into one of the leather recliners in the living room. "How are your legs?"

"Still there? Still useless?" Jude glared at him. "Don't use my issues as a distraction."

"Your issues aren't a distraction, Jude." Mack leaned forward and pointed the beer at him. "How are you doing?"

Shrugging, Jude seemed to struggle to answer the question. Mack tried never to compare their situations, but his greatest fear was losing his ability to move around freely. Something his closest friend now had to deal with on a daily basis.

"Think you'll regain the use of your legs?" Mack never pressed Jude, but they'd always promised honesty to each other.

"Fuck if I know."

Dragging the cold beer across his forehead, Mack took a long swig of it. He had to get into Toshiro's good books again. They usually made up fairly quickly after one of their disagreements.

"Rafe's a slimy git."

Mack couldn't necessarily disagree given how the fault for the incident that caused Jude to lose the use of his legs could be laid at Rafe's feet. "I know you—"

"Save it," Jude cut him off sharply.

"Jude."

His mate pointed a finger at him in warning. "You listen to me, you stupid wanker with too many names, I kept my mouth shut to avoid starting shit, but Tosh's right, man. Rafe's a sneaky son of a dog shit."

"Son of a dog shit?" Mack snorted beer through his nose. "Fuck that hurt."

"My mum didn't raise me to use foul language." Jude winked at him. "Just tell Tosh you're sorry and he's right."

"Because he is?"

"Because you're tired of wanking." Jude saluted him with his beer. "And he's usually right."

Mack flipped him off, sulking into his beer. "Not always."

"Once a year isn't a brilliant record, mate." Jude manoeuvred his way across the room towards his set up of laptops. "The tiara made it safely to the museum."

"No connections to us?"

"None at all." Jude gave him an affronted scowl. "How many years have I handled the return of stolen items to unsuspecting owners? I know what I'm doing even if my legs aren't what they used to be."

"*Jude.*"

"Got feeling in my toe."

"Really?" Mack knew the doctors had told Jude there was the slimmest of possibilities of his regaining some use of his legs. They'd warned him not to count on it. "All the work you're doing paying off, then?"

"Fuck I hope so. I've sunk a lot of my earnings from our years working together on every newfangled therapy out there. I'm not giving up." Jude grabbed one of his laptops and brought it over. "Found a new potential job for us."

Setting his drink aside, Mack read through a news article about a recent theft from a reclusive billionaire. Jude leaned over to switch tabs to a message about a hefty reward offered for any news leading to the return. He didn't know if it was large enough to be worth the effort.

"Know who did it?"

"Shipton."

"You're shitting me." Mack had no qualms about getting one over on Mary Shipton. "You sure?"

"Seen her Instagram?"

Mack pinched the bridge of his nose, breathing out noisily. "Seriously? She can't be that stupid. I know she's not that idiotic. Rafe wouldn't have anything to do with her if she was."

Jude flipped to yet another tab on his browser. "She did."

There in all her pale, blonde-haired, blue-eyed glory stood Mary Shipton, looking more model than thief. Mack immediately spotted a familiar bracelet on her slender wrist.

She apparently was idiotic or arrogant enough to not be concerned about putting stolen property on display for the entire world to see.

How the hell hasn't Rafe ripped her a new one for this?

In his experience, his mentor had always insisted on any property being moved almost immediately. Holding on to stolen goods tended to raise the risk of getting caught with it. Rafe generally managed to skilfully avoid those situations.

"Someone should probably teach her a lesson about flaunting her success." Jude grinned at him, teeth gleaming more like a shark than anything else. "Want her address?"

"Why don't I take my infirm grandfather for a walk in the park sometime this week?" Mack knew she went for a daily run not far from her flat. "Up for it?"

"Why do I always have to play the old man?" Jude grabbed his laptop out of Mack's hands. "You're jealous of my looks."

"On what planet?"

"People tell me I look like David Beckham's doppelganger."

"Your mum doesn't count." Mack refused to admit the truth of his friend's statement. "Do you want to help or not?"

"Fine. *Wanker*."

"Brilliant. First, I have to get Toshi talking to me again." Mack massaged his forehead to stave off a sudden headache.

"Suck his cock."

"*Jude.*"

"What? It'd work for me." Jude raised his hand to stop Mack from responding to him. "Not if you sucked my cock…. You know what, there is no fixing the phrasing. Just go home and enjoy your man. He always forgives you."

The "everyone always forgives you" was left unspoken. For not being Irish, Mack had enough luck for him to want to search through his ancestry. He always tended to come out on top, rare in their world for someone who chose to never walk over others to succeed.

"Your sight is getting worse." Jude tossed the comment out so casually it took Mack a moment to process. "Dominica mentioned your driving in Italy was more shit than normal, especially at night."

Mack got to his feet, turning towards the door. "Have to go. Promised to visit my dad."

"What? You're actually making the two-hour trek out to Worcestershire? A bit late in the day to get started, isn't it?" Jude guided his chair over to block Mack's escape. "What's your plan then? Wait until it's too late to make a difference in your sight?"

Unlike with his husband or other family, Mack couldn't evade Jude's concern quite so quickly. It felt like spitting in the face of his friend's own troubles. He baulked at showing his lifelong friend such disrespect.

If Jude refuses to allow his paralysis to hold him back, how can I give up without even trying?

"What are you so fucking afraid of?" Jude rested his hand on Mack's arm. His fingers were still clamped around the knob of the front door, itching for an escape. "What's the absolute worst thing that could happen to you?"

"I'll be blind," Mack whispered hoarsely. He released

the knob before he hurt himself. "What good is a blind thief to anyone?"

"Seriously?" Jude let his arm go, gliding his chair over to the side more. "I'm likely never to walk again. Has it changed how *useful* I am to you?"

"Don't be daft." Mack dropped his forehead against the door. "Robin Hood didn't lose his sight. Pirates don't go stumbling around in the dark on their ships on the high seas."

"They do with high levels of rum," Jude pointed out helpfully. "Your obsession with this image of who we are and what we do has messed your head up, mate."

"Trying to say I've gone around the bend?"

"No, you prat." Jude drove forward over Mack's foot with one of the wheels. "I'm saying you bought into your own made-up vision that we're some sort of sodding superheros."

"Haven't."

"Have."

"Haven't," Mack muttered petulantly. He flipped Jude off with both middle fingers. "Quit backing up over my toes."

"You have." Jude went over them once more before heading down the hall. "I'd think you'd want to deal with facts rather than stumble around blindly on what might be happening to you."

Pun intended?

Or is it more of a mic drop?

That's what Nico calls it, right?

Drop the mick?

Drop the mic?

Oh my fucking God.

I'm an old man.

"If you're done with your crisis, why don't we finish our beers and you can mope into yours while we figure out how we're going to ruin Shipton's day," Jude called out from the living room. "Besides, you're supposed to visit your dad tomorrow—not today."

"Wanker."

"Can't feel that either," Jude retorted.

"Suddenly going blind doesn't seem quite so shit." Mack hadn't considered how the injury to his back had affected his friend's body outside of his legs. "Maybe you should have my beer as well."

"And you're still an idiot."

CHAPTER TEN

TOSHIRO

The sexiest thing in the world was Mack with his reading glasses. No question. Toshiro watched him over the top of his book. His husband had gotten lost in the biography of one of his favourite biographers.

A ping on his nearby laptop drew his attention away from pretending to read. Toshiro snatched it from the coffee table, opening it to check the email. His translator friend had come through for them on interpreting the two sets of documents found at the villa in the chapel and safe.

The subject line, in particular, caught his immediate attention: *what the hell have you two stepped into this time?* Toshiro scanned through one of the attachments to the email. He immediately understood what had his friend so concerned; while the papers in the chapel were from at least a century before, the ones in the safe proved far more recent.

In the last month or so, they'd seen a few news articles

about the theft of antiquities. Aside from Pierce's warning, Toshiro had already wondered how deeply it went. They hadn't heard many rumours in their own circles about it—concerning in and of itself.

Each attachment contained concrete proof of the existence of a pipeline of stolen antiquities being moved from Syria, Iraq, and Afghanistan through the Ukraine and eventually into France and England. Toshiro read one of the lists of items in one of the shipments that included statues, jewellery, and coins. *Lots of coins.* The melted-down gold bars suddenly made more sense to him.

If you can't sell gold coins, melt them down and launder them that way.

"Mack?" He nudged his husband with his bare foot to draw his attention away from his e-reader. "You'll want to have a look at this."

Mack set the tablet to one side and hopped across the table to drop on the couch next to him. His reading glasses slipped on his nose slightly when he bent forward to see the laptop screen better. "Shit. What Pandora's Box have we gone and opened now?"

"A large, dangerously lucrative one." Toshiro tabbed to yet another image, slowly going through all of them. He decided not to mention how it might all be linked to a current Interpol investigation. One issue at a time. Mack and his uncle hadn't talked in ages; now didn't seem the right moment to bring it up. "We could always pretend we never saw it."

"Or?" Mack set his glasses on the edge of the couch,

ignoring how they slid to the floor. "We'd earn a fair bit of coin from the rewards listed for some of them. It's not as if we've never tracked down the spoils of war."

"True enough." Toshiro went to the last screen. "It's a bit scary how no names are listed—not even the one we know for certain."

After forwarding the email to Charlie, Dom, and Jude for their input, Toshiro placed the laptop on the table and bent down to retrieve the discarded glasses. He stared at them for a second; the only physical evidence of Mack's degrading sight. They were the only proof of it since his husband went out of his way to avoid any others.

"Don't." Mack laid a hand over his, easing the glasses away from him. "I know. I know what you want to say, but I'm not ready yet."

His heart ached for the man he'd loved since their teens. Ready or not, Retinitis Pigmentosa had no cure. His sight would continue to grow progressively worse. Denial did nothing to stop it.

For three years, Toshiro had watched with growing concern while Mack struggled with worsening night blindness. They'd always thought the genetic disorder was a problem for the future. He'd hoped perhaps his husband might be one of the rare lucky ones.

Reading glasses, shades for bright days, and regular contacts staved off the inevitable. The night blindness had been a new trouble to add to the list of signs. One that threatened Mack's ability to pretend everything else he'd managed to live with was ordinary.

"Gregor." Toshiro shifted on the cushion to face him. His fingers tangled up with his husband's. "You can't run from this forever."

"Why not?"

"You're going blind, love. You'll run into something." He grinned at Mack, who gave a watery chuckle. "I'd prefer you not break anything important."

"My face?"

"Your cock." Toshiro purposefully turned the conversation to a lighter tone. "It's incredibly important to me."

"Arse." Mack twisted around to stretch out on the sofa with his head in Toshiro's lap. "I won't ignore it forever."

Toshiro dropped his fingers into his husband's dark, wavy hair. He often wished Mack would grow it out to reveal the curls more. "You're stubborn enough to give it a damn good try, though."

"Jude says he can feel one of his toes."

"Another of our merry band of misfits who's stubborn enough to give ignoring doctor's orders a damn good try." Toshiro found a burst of hope shoot through him at the news. "Just one toe?"

"Give it a week. Jude lives to work miracles." Mack tilted his head back to smile up at him. "Don't know how he finds the courage to face each day."

"What choice does he have?" Toshiro remembered asking his sister once how she dealt with all her struggles as an autistic. She'd rolled her eyes at him before reminding him that her only other choice would've been to hide in her room until she got old and wrinkled. "You live your life, or you allow everything to pass you by. Jude's never been good at sitting back while everyone else continues on."

"True enough." Mack closed his eyes with a tired sigh. "You going to the prison with me tomorrow?"

"Have to go see Charlie."

"You just don't want to drive two hours," Mack whinged.

Also true.

The following morning, Mack headed up to South Littleton in Worcestershire to visit with his father. Toshiro left the quiet of the loft to see his sister. He cycled the thirty minutes over to her little house.

Toshiro locked his bike up to the gate and headed back to find Dom sculpting in the garden. "Is she having a verbal or a non-verbal day?"

"Non-ish?" Dom rested her hands on her knees. "Your mum played helicopter all morning. It frayed my angel's nerves as always."

"She means well."

"She means your sister well right into a meltdown," Dom snapped. Her fingers dug into her statue, ruining it. "She's in her music room—probably pounding away on the piano to relieve the tension."

"Mind if I go in?" Toshiro gestured towards the back door to their small house. "See if I can coax her out."

"Go on then." Dom returned to her mess of clay. "Get her to eat something, will you? She skipped breakfast."

Once inside, Toshiro easily heard the soulful melody coming from the second floor. He followed the strains of

Beethoven up to the closed door. Grabbing his phone, he sent a quick text to Charlie, since knocking would likely make things worse for her.

Charlie: It's open.

Stepping into the room, Toshiro found his twin sister sitting at her upright piano. Her little Norfolk Terrier, Bach, lay beside her on the cushioned bench. The dog never strayed far from Charlie, acting as a barometer for her stress levels. Whenever Charlie left town, he stayed with their mum, who spoiled her only grandchild.

Bach came into their lives after they discovered Charlie had extraordinarily high blood pressure. Her doctor had suggested she work to find ways to alleviate her stress. The small terrier they'd found through a rescue organisation fit the bill perfectly.

On good days, Bach tended to play like any slightly manic terrier. On Charlie's quiet days, he curled up at her side. He seemed to know when she'd teetered on the edge of a meltdown, and helped her with it.

In her twenties, Charlie had been diagnosed with high blood pressure. Aside from stress relief, the doctor told them he believed many autistics suffered from elevated stress from merely living in a non-autistic world with all the constant input. *No shit.* His twin had initially panicked before settling down to try to do her best to fix the situation.

Setting boundaries for her and us.

In a twist of irony, the blood pressure situation actually led to Charlie becoming more comfortable in her autistic skin. She stopped playing the game of trying to fit in.

Toshiro had never been more proud of his twin, even if at times it made life more difficult.

Toshiro sat on the floor near the piano, not behind her but within her line of sight. "Want to talk?"

"Mummy." She tapped her finger repeatedly against the middle C note while petting Bach with her other hand. "She knows I'm in my thirties, right?"

"Probably." Toshiro loved their mum, but she often tried to baby both of them. Charlie took it more personally than he did. She'd had to struggle harder for her independence. "Think it's her way of dealing with missing us."

"I'm not helpless." Charlie banged on a few keys. "Not helpless or stupid or useless."

Toshiro shuffled forward until he could offer Charlie a hug, smiling when she fell into his arms to accept it. "I'm sorry. I know it doesn't help to know she loves us. But I know you're not helpless, stupid, or useless. And I'll talk to mum about boundaries."

"Again."

Truth be told, their mum had for a long time come over to his place without warning or even knocking. She'd only stopped after walking in on him and Mack enjoying a late morning together. He had a feeling Charlie might not appreciate his offering it as a suggestion to help her.

"Again. I'll do it until she gets it. She loves us, but that doesn't mean she should steamroll over you." He allowed Charlie to scoot away from his embrace. "How about I whip up some soft eggs with toast soldiers? It's your favourite."

One of their favourite childhood comfort foods, slivers

of buttered toast that dipped perfectly into a boiled egg with a runny yolk. Charlie had been known to eat it for breakfast, lunch, and dinner on her stressed days. She still had the egg cup that their grandmother gave her as a gift for her first birthday.

"Ready? Or do you need more time alone with my furry nephew?" Toshiro scratched the terrier behind the ear. "Did grandmum bring you anything?"

Charlie snickered at him but pointed to a basket on top of the piano. "More treats and toys. He's never going to play with all of them."

A bark from Bach appeared to indicate his strong disagreement. The twins laughed together for a moment at his antics. Charlie led him down the stairs to the small kitchen at the back of the house.

"One or two eggs?" Toshiro rummaged around in their tiny fridge to find the eggs and butter. "Pop the toast in, will you?"

They ate in quiet. A familiar silence he'd always enjoyed with his twin. Charlie went through her eggs, and then one of his.

Typical.

Setting his plate on the floor for Bach to lick clean, Toshiro considered another cup of coffee. He'd planned on talking to Charlie and Dom about the Pierce problem. *Now's probably not the best time for it. Shit. We're all a bunch of procrastinators.*

"Jude told me about his plan to steal from Mary, Mary, Quite Contrary."

Toshiro set his mug down slowly, staring at his sister. "What plan to steal from Mary Shipton?"

"Didn't Mack tell you?" Charlie's eyes widened. "Bugger."

"No, he hasn't mentioned any plans. What'd Jude say?" Toshiro made a mental note to punish his husband when he returned from his prison visit. "C'mon, Charlie. You can't tease me with a hint."

"Need more toast." Charlie bolted from the table over to drop more bread in the toaster. "Ask Jude."

"Oh, I'll be asking someone." He'd already made a mental outline of all the ways to torment Mack until he spilt the beans. "And that someone will definitely be telling me what I want to know."

"Bugger."

CHAPTER ELEVEN

MACK

The drive out to South Littleton always went far more quickly than the journey home. Mack usually left the prison with a heavy heart. His father grew frailer with each passing year, and he dreaded the inevitable call about his death.

In his memories, Mack still saw his father as a healthy, vibrant man who'd laughed louder than anyone in a room. He'd told tall tales with a smidge of truth to them. Not perfect by any stretch of the imagination, his dad had done his best for his son.

It grew harder to make the trip. Not only had his father lost weight, but his sight had almost completely gone as well. Mack wondered if there was any point in attempting yet another petition for his release from prison on account of his failing health.

Halfway home, Mack had to pull off the motorway. He stopped on the side of the road, resting his head against the steering wheel. Gut instinct told him his father likely wouldn't survive long enough for him to even get the petition written.

Mack fished his phone out of his pocket to call Toshiro but changed his mind. He scrolled through the contacts on his list until he found one of his other family members. *What the fuck am I doing? It's ringing.*

"Siddall."

Mack forced himself to speak over the lump in his throat. "It's Gregor."

"Can you hang on a minute?" His uncle sounded completely stunned on the other end of the line. "Just—give me a second here."

"Sure." Mack dropped his forehead against the steering wheel again, listening to muffled voices and finally the sound of a door being shut. "I can call later."

"You won't," Pierce said, slightly breathless. "Is everything okay? Toshiro fine?"

"Saw my dad today."

"Ah, yes." Pierce cleared his throat loudly before continuing. "He's not doing well."

Understatement of the sodding year.

"Don't know why I called you." Mack sat up, rubbing his hand across his face. "I was an arse when we spoke last."

"I wasn't much better."

And he hadn't been.

Mack adjusted his seat belt, fidgeting in all honesty, something entirely out of the ordinary for him. *Just ask, you twat.* "You still in Manchester?"

"London at the moment." His uncle sounded amused,

but Mack couldn't figure out why.

"I'm thirty minutes from home. Could you meet me for tea somewhere? Maybe a very late lunch?" Mack wanted to hang up and forget everything. He found himself in the strange position of wanting family to reach out to touch without the interference of prison guards. "Toshiro's not expecting me; he'll probably be chuffed to know I called you."

Another awkward silence followed. Mack had the sneaking suspicion his uncle had given up on them ever meeting again—outside of an arrest warrant. He hoped this wouldn't all blow up in his face.

"Monmouth coffee? Or do you want something more substantial?" Pierce broke the quiet. "There's a decent café not far from Monmouth that offers more than pastries and cake."

Agreeing to meet up at the café, Mack had plenty of time in traffic to consider the monumental mistake he'd made. Toshiro would be proud of him. His husband had subtly encouraged him to reach out to his uncle for a while before letting the subject drop.

Traffic cleared just as Mack had started to change his mind. He decided not to take the cowardly way out of not showing up. His pulse raced more than it ever did on a heist.

"Going to get out of the car?"

Mack jumped in his seat, turning towards his open driver-side window to find his uncle watching him. "I was thinking about it."

"Want me to leave?" His uncle waited patiently for him

to make his decision.

In social situations, Toshiro handled silences far better than Mack. He tended to fill the quiet with chatter. It ran in the family, as he'd always been told his mum could talk the ear off anyone.

Sitting across from him, Mack honestly had no idea what possessed him to call his uncle. He certainly had no idea what to say to the man now. Pierce just seemed to find it all very amusing.

The bastard.

"Is this your husband's doing?" Pierce gestured between them. "Never imagined he'd speak to you about contacting me."

"He didn't." Mack narrowed his eyes at his uncle. "What does Toshi have to do with anything?"

"I just assumed when you called that he'd mentioned our getting together." Pierce winced as the realisation clearly hit him Mack hadn't known. "Right. He'll be chuffed I narked on him then."

"He will." Mack chuckled darkly. He had every intention of using it to his advantage. It wasn't often he managed to get one over on Toshiro. "Saw my dad today."

"So you mentioned on the phone." Pierce rested his arms on the table with his fingers wrapped around his cup of tea. "How is he? I'd heard his health was failing."

Mack detected no malice in the words. His uncle and his father had never gotten along—particularly after Pierce decided on life as a police officer. "If I'm honest with myself, I'm not entirely certain how much longer he's got."

"Can I help?"

"You want to help my dad?" Mack asked incredulously. "Didn't you tell him to rot in hell?"

"My sister had just died. He got caught up in the theft of a painting that led to two people being shot to death." Pierce whacked his palm against the table, drawing a scolding tut from a passing waitress. "Whatever pirates may have done in the past along our ancestry line, we've no place for murderers in our family."

"So why are you even here?" Mack refused to rehash the same argument yet again. "Why bother?"

If Mack knew anything for sure, he knew his father had never been involved in killing someone. They'd had this conversation the last time they met. It had been far more volatile, though. Seeing the frailty of his father had shaken him a bit; his desire to fight had gone right out of the window.

"I *have* plenty of space in my family for my only nephew." Pierce seemed to suddenly deflate; the look in his eyes turned sad. "Whatever he's done, I imagine your dad would like to spend his last days with his son."

"He would." Mack appreciated the olive branch his uncle clearly wanted to offer. "I'll be making the drive out more if the prison will let me. They don't always after the riots they had."

Pierce stirred his tea for a few seconds. "I'll see if I can help you with it. I doubt I can influence his release one way or the other, but I might be able to either get you in to see him more often or maybe even get him moved closer to London. He's no danger to anyone at this point."

He was never a sodding danger to anyone.

Breathe, Mack.

He released a breath and allowed his anger to go with it. "Thank you."

CHAPTER TWELVE

"What's this about a plan to steal a bracelet?" Toshiro grinned at his husband across the breakfast table the following morning. He'd managed to hold his tongue when Mack had come home looking as though the world weighed on his shoulders. "You and Jude trying to cut us out?"

Mack paused in the middle of spreading marmalade on a piece of toast. "Hmm. What's this about you sneaking off to have coffee with my uncle?"

Shit.

Busted.

A glob of marmalade caught him on the left cheek. Toshiro narrowed his eyes at his husband who had another teaspoon of ammunition at the ready. He held up a piece of toast just in time to catch it.

Dropping it onto his plate, Toshiro reached past the pot of honey to grab the beans. They'd gone for a full English breakfast—a rare treat for them. He dug his fingers in to get a handful to launch at Mack, hitting him on the chest.

The war turned brutal. Every piece of their breakfast became fuel for their battle. They eventually ran out of ammo with food dripping from themselves and the table.

"Truce?" Mack offered with a grin.

"Fine. *Truce.*" Toshiro swiped at his face to clear the egg from it. "Think we might want to clean up a bit."

"Maybe." He grabbed a piece of toast to drag it through the marmalade on his cheek and took a bite. "We could always eat it clean."

Toshiro pinched the bridge of his nose. "No, no we couldn't."

Cleaning up took longer than making breakfast twice. Toshiro wasn't entirely satisfied they'd gotten all of the bits of egg. He'd have to bring Bach over from his sister's to have him hoover it all up.

"Are you going to tell me about the bracelet?" Toshiro pinned his husband against the kitchen counter where he'd been washing up the dishes, having lost their coin toss. "This piece of jewellery you've decided to nick from Rafe's new protégé."

"Protégé, my arse." Mack twisted around with his hands dripping with suds. He wiped them dry on Toshiro's shirt. "She's an immature twat."

"Says the man who wants to steal a bracelet from her simply because he doesn't like her." Toshiro grimaced down at his now soapy shirt. "I've already changed once this morning, *stronzo.*"

"Why can't you just say arsehole? Why do you have to

find new languages to say it in?" Mack slipped his hands underneath Toshiro's damp shirt. "Try it? *Arsehole.*"

"Italian sounds better." Toshiro shrugged.

"Much prefer French." Mack leaned forward to lick Toshiro's lip, sucking his bottom one into his mouth. "Maybe you should change again. Slowly. So I can enjoy it."

"Not enough time. You wasted all our extra time with a food fight." Toshiro smiled against his husband's mouth, having to ignore the way his cock twitched at Mack's tongue continuing to press for entrance. "*Gregor.*"

His husband's hands slipped down his abdomen, fingernails scratching against his skin. Toshiro inhaled sharply when Mack shoved a hand into his trousers to take a hold of his shaft. They really hadn't the time to indulge, given the crew could walk into their loft at any moment.

"What are you doing?" He tried to pull away, which only slid his cock through Mack's warm, calloused fingers. "We can't. We've already scarred them for life several times over."

"We'll have to be quick." Mack stroked him firmly, refusing to release him.

"We're getting too old to be quick. Can you believe we're in our thirties?" Toshiro laughed when Mack glared at him. "Or maybe being fast is a sign of how old we are getting."

Before Mack could respond, the new chime they'd gotten to signal their loft front door opening sounded. Toshiro yanked his husband's hand out of his trousers. He grabbed a towel to wipe his shirt dry as best he could.

"If you're fucking in the kitchen again, I'm suing you for emotional distress," Dom called from the hallway. "Charlie's waiting for Jude downstairs to help him up."

When Jude had his accident, they'd decided to splurge on getting an elevator installed into their two-storey building. Mack had come up with the idea. They'd done it as a surprise, which their friend appeared to appreciate after he'd cursed them for making him weepy.

"How's she going to help him up?"

"It's Charlie. She's fascinated by your elevator, but we don't really have to use it, do we?" Dom joined them in the kitchen. She immediately made herself at home, pulling out two mugs. "Got coffee brewing?"

"You know where everything is." Toshiro left them in the kitchen to find a dry shirt. He hated the feeling of a shirt plastered to his chest, especially by lukewarm water.

Once everyone had arrived, the group sat down to brainstorm ideas. Jude and Mack wanted to immediately begin work on tracking down the items listed on the documents from the villa. Toshiro suggested a bit of restraint to avoid any risks of going head-to-head with an incredibly dangerous man.

With a fair amount of good-natured bickering, the group managed to settle on their schedule for the next month. They'd tackle the bracelet first since Mack had become obsessed with it. Toshiro hadn't been able to talk him out of it.

And he'd tried.

For a reason Toshiro couldn't identify, Mary Shipton continually antagonised Mack, occasionally even on purpose. She had some sort of agenda that had become obvious over the last year. Toshiro wanted nothing to do with the drama, but his husband couldn't help himself.

Part of it came from family pride; the Shiptons and the Eastons traced their family lines deeply into the history of piracy in Europe. Rumour had it that one had managed the downfall of the other at one point, starting a bitter rivalry. They'd never found any concrete proof of it.

The youngest member of the Shipton clan had come onto the scene out of nowhere. They'd never even heard of the brat until a year or so ago. Toshiro wished she'd disappear back where she came from.

Her focus on Mack worried him. She'd tried to join their crew initially, which had proved a disaster. When she turned up as Rafe's new protégé next, Toshiro had wondered if there was more to her agenda than first imagined.

Dom tapped him subtly on the side of the leg, leaning in to whisper under her breath, "Fifty quid says this goes horribly wrong for all involved."

"Done." He had a feeling he'd taken a losing bet.

Oh well.

Toshiro wanted the conversation to move on from petty thefts from rivals to the more treacherous job of returning antiquities to the right museums and countries. "What about the gold bars?"

"Nico promised they'd arrive in a few days. They drove a rather convoluted route up across a few extra countries to prevent being traced to any of us. We'll keep a few back and sell the rest of them." Charlie read a few details from a text from their beloved Nico. "He'll let us know when they've gotten here safely."

The gold bars they'd discovered in Italy had been a bit too conspicuous to try to sneak through airport customs. Nico had the ingenious plan to use a few of his most trusted friends to make the drive, earning themselves a bit of coin in the process. They'd drop some of it off along the way to sell.

Just in case they get stopped, at least we won't risk losing all of it.

They only made that mistake once. It had been a painfully expensive one. One that almost got them all locked up for a few years.

And that would've been a very bad day.

"Tosh?"

He glanced up at Jude. "Sorry. What?"

"Statue, jewellery, coins, or documents?" Jude had his laptop sitting on his knees facing the group. "I've picked the ones that stand out the most; it'll make them easier to track."

"Nothing too big to get out." Dom winked at Toshiro, clearly remembering the time they'd made the mistake of taking a contract to return a painting. It had been too large to even fit on top of their vehicle. "Right, Mack?"

"What?" He glared at all of them when they snickered. "You write measurements down wrong one bloody time, and no one lets you forget it."

"Ten inches to ten feet. Bit of a difference." Dom looped

her arm around Charlie's shoulder when she settled next to her. "Took five of us to walk it covered in sheets across a city. I still say we should've won an award for stupidest crooks in London."

CHAPTER THIRTEEN

MACK

"Why exactly have we blown through a massive amount of our heist budget to stay at Claridge's for a week?" Toshiro bounced on the plush mattress in one of the rooms of their penthouse at the luxury hotel. "Aside from your wanting to indulge some bizarre Little Lord Fauntleroy fantasy."

"Why? Want to be my stable boy?" Mack wiggled his eyebrows at his husband. "Or my butler? I already have the perfect uniform in mind."

"Birthday suit?"

"My favourite." Mack threw himself onto the bed beside Toshiro. "I'm not playing lord of the manor. Jude thinks one of the dealers at Grays Antique might be involved. We're going to play a wealthy gay couple on the hunt to furnish our country estate."

"Our country estate?" Toshiro shoved him on the shoulder, sending him tumbling off the bed to the floor. "I assume this is why we had a delivery of luggage that I'd never seen before."

Mack leaned up on his elbows to point towards one of the garment bags. "Suits. Several of them. Dom called in a favour from one of her stylist friends. Ready to dazzle London?"

"A week at Claridge's, throwing money around, and eating out at fancy restaurants? Sounds like the honeymoon that we never got around to taking." Toshiro crawled over to the edge of the bed to grin down at Mack. "We should clean up before dinner."

"Sunken bathtub?"

"Sunken bathtub."

Smiling devilishly at his husband, Mack got quickly to his feet. He grabbed the hem of his long-sleeved T-shirt and dragged it over his head. Toshiro followed him across the room towards the large bathroom while they left a trail of clothes behind them.

Mack got the water going then turned around to admire his husband's naked flesh where he leaned casually against the sink. "We've seven days to figure out things at the market—and to christen every surface in this suite, leave our mark on the penthouse for all the toffs who come for a stay in the future."

Toshiro hopped up on the sink; he used his leg to hook Mack to pull him closer. "Think you're up for it?"

Mack shoved Toshiro's legs apart and pressed up between them. "Are you?"

Toshiro shifted on the sink. "Not sure this thing is sturdy enough for us. I'd rather not wind up with shards of marble in my arse and having to explain the damage to the concierge."

"Right. Marble up the arse would be bad." Mack couldn't help chuckling at the visual of trying to talk their way into an innocent reason. He glanced over his shoulder to see the water had quickly risen in the tub. "Bath it is."

After Toshiro slipped off the marble counter, Mack reached down to grasp his husband's semi-hard shaft. He gently led him across to the bubbling water in the Jacuzzi tub. They slipped into the warmth, facing each other on their knees.

The water lapped against their skin. Mack enjoyed the slightly pleasurable jolt from the bubbles drifting across his body, and in particular his erection. It took him from hardening to completely erect incredibly quickly.

His fingers slid easily over Toshiro's water-slicked body. Mack flicked first one nipple ring then the other. He'd always enjoyed the stark contrast of the silver against his husband's golden-toned skin.

Suds dripped down both of their chests. Toshiro slipped his hands along Mack's sides, shuffling forward on his knees until their shafts bumped together. They bounced on the frothing water, creating an extra level of sensation for both of them.

Mack slid his hand up Toshiro's chest, along his neck, back into his hair. He gripped the silken strands firmly to tilt his husband's head. "Are you going to take me in the marble tub?"

The dark gleam in Toshiro's eyes told him that he was

in for a wild ride. Mack stretched an arm out to snag his toiletry bag sitting on a nearby shelf. He'd made sure to pack several types of lube, including a water-soluble one for just this occasion.

What's the Cubs' motto?

Always be prepared?

Or is that the Yank Scouts' one?

Setting the tube on the edge of the tub, Mack returned his fingers to Toshiro's hair. He had a slight obsession with it. His hands always seemed to find a way to use the soft, straight strands to guide his husband into a kiss.

He'd wished several times that Toshiro would grow it out. His husband had gone through a period where he kept his hair almost down to his arse. He'd braid it in intricate designs that managed to make him even manlier than before.

Mack had loved it.

"You're thinking about my long hair again, aren't you?" Toshiro splashed water up into his face and drew his thoughts away from the lovely memories of how he'd used the long braid during sex. "Sometimes you're a right kinky bastard."

"Never heard you complain." Mack brought his hand down to grip Toshiro's shaft, stroking him firmly. "Going to start whinging about it now?"

"Going to start something." Toshiro shifted back, stretching his legs out in the tub on either side of Mack, who edged forward to kneel, so he easily straddled his husband. "Are we done teasing, Gregor?"

Definitely.

Mack grabbed the lube and shifted up on his knees to prepare himself. Toshiro breathed heavily beneath him while his gaze zeroed in on Mack's fingers.

With a roguish smile, Toshiro bent forward to reach around to grip Mack's hands. He used the hold to control the thrusting of his husband's lubed fingers. *How the bloody hell does he always manage to send my already racing heart into the stratosphere?*

His patience evaporated with each twist of the fingers. Mack drew both their hands away from him and eased up only to skilfully lower himself onto Toshiro's erection. He enjoyed the slight burn as he pushed himself down onto the familiar embrace.

He wound his arms around Toshiro. Their chests rubbed together, causing his husband's piercing to brush against his skin. Their lips met in a series of hard, breath-stealing kisses.

The water lapped warmly around their rocking bodies. Mack spread his legs out further to allow Toshiro to drive up into him a bit deeper. Their groans were muffled by each other's mouths.

Kiss.

Lift up.

Kiss.

Drop down.

It was obviously the perfect recipe to drive him insane. Mack scratched his fingers along Toshiro's back, up to once again tangle in his hair. He yanked back to allow his lips to drift down to his husband's neck, which he immediately teased with licks and bites.

While his husband muttered in Italian, Mack ignored him to focus on controlling his movements. It became increasingly difficult with Toshiro reaching between them to stroke his shaft. His thumb drifted around the head of his cock before he took hold of it with his entire hand.

The addition of Toshiro stroking his cock sent him over the edge. Mack picked up the force of his movements. It didn't take long for them to officially christen the first surface in the penthouse.

"*Fuck.*" Mack collapsed against Toshiro, allowing the water to wash away the mess on their abdomens. "You're… something… brilliant."

"And you're never as eloquent as you are with my cock up your arse." Toshiro dropped his head back against the edge of the tub. "It was brilliant, though."

By the time they left their room, it was already well into the evening. Mack strained to see in the glare of the lights. He tried as always to hide it, but his shoe caught the kerb, almost sending him sprawling to the ground.

"Gregor." Toshiro threw his arm around his shoulder, guiding him through a group of people towards the restaurant where they planned to eat. Their route took them past Grays, which would allow them a quick glance at their target. "Slow down. Walking faster won't change your sight."

"Don't." He didn't want to break down. They had a cover to maintain. "Not now, Toshi."

Toshiro used his hold on him to drag him away from the

door of the restaurant, around the corner and away from the milling groups on the pavement. "Then when? We can't ignore this forever, Gregor. I love you. I *love* you. We said vows to each other. Remember? We promised to always be honest with each other. We swore to lift one another up in our darkest moments. I'm tired of pretending your sight isn't changing. If we tiptoe around this, you'll lose everything without ever knowing if you might've done something to improve things."

Mack dragged a hand roughly through his hair. He turned his head away to avoid the raw pain and tears in his husband's eyes. "Toshi."

"We took vows, Gregor. Do you not trust me to carry this weight with you?" Toshiro punched Mack lightly in the chest, pushing him back into the brick wall. "Don't shut me out."

Making his husband cry was on the top of the list of things Mack went out of his way to avoid. He hated knowing he'd put the tears in Toshiro's eyes. They stood silently on the pavement for almost a full minute.

Mack grabbed Toshiro into a hug and clung to him almost desperately. "Not trying to shut you out. I swear to fucking God, it's never been about not trusting you."

Toshiro bent his head until their foreheads rested together. "When did it become you against the world instead of us?"

"I'm afraid." Mack struggled to get the words out. "What if it doesn't stop with night blindness?"

"We'll find out together," Toshiro promised.

"Fine." Mack brought his hands up to rest on Toshiro's

shoulders on either side of his neck. His thumbs brushed against the skin above his starched shirt and jacket collar. *"Fine."*

I can't run anymore.

CHAPTER FOURTEEN

TOSHIRO

After their emotional moment, Toshiro hadn't quite felt ready to face the restaurant they'd gotten reservations at. Mack hadn't needed much convincing to return to Claridge's. Room service would be just as good, if not better.

They wound up sitting on comfortable chairs on the terrace to enjoy the clear night sky. Toshiro had changed into boxers and one of the lush bathrobes left for them. Mack snickered every time he flashed him.

The in-room dining menu required a good twenty minutes of perusal before they could decide on what to enjoy. Toshiro usually preferred not to waste money on frivolous things. He'd winced at the prices, but knew their cover required a careless attitude to the cost.

It came as no surprise that Mack had no trouble with the prices. His husband had always enjoyed the finer things in life, even when he couldn't afford them. One of their rare points of contention came from their different approaches to handling finances.

"Steak?" Mack flung a piece at him. "I can understand why Rafe wastes so much of his money at hotels like this. He spends more time in luxury suites than he does his mansion."

"Can we have a Rafe-less evening? I'd prefer not to have indigestion." Toshiro paused to finish the bite of Mack's sirloin before returning to his own lamb cutlets. "This is damn good."

The indulgent meal wowed them into silence. Toshiro enjoyed the succulent meat as much as his husband, the quiet punctuated periodically with hums of pleasure.

Mack held up the bowl that contained a dark chocolate crémeux with ganache. "Think anyone can see us up here?"

"Not really, not if we dim the lights further." Toshiro eyed his husband suspiciously. "What's going on in your sick, twisted mind?"

Mack dipped a finger in the pot before slowly sucking it clean of the warm chocolate pudding. "Wouldn't you like to lick this off me?"

"You—or your cock?"

"Oh, I like the way you think. Chocolate-covered penis." Mack broke out into a smile. "Yours, mine, or both?"

"Chocolate-y sixty-nine on the terrace?" Toshiro made a mental note to leave a large tip for the cleaning staff who'd be responsible for their mess. *I almost feel sorry enough not to do it. Almost.* "Both. Do you have enough pudding for it?"

"Your cock's not that big."

"Big enough to have you screaming my name." Toshiro flicked a piece of his apple from his poached apple and white chocolate mousse at Mack. "Big enough to fill you up."

While Mack darted inside to turn off several of the lights, Toshiro shoved his bathrobe off. He shimmied out of his boxers and eyed the mousse in the bowl nearby. Grabbing the dish, he dumped the lot of it on his chest.

Weirdly warm and moist.

Toshiro was contemplating licking himself clean with the scent of chocolate making his mouth water when a thud followed by a curse drew his attention away from his sudden edibleness. "Forget to leave a light on so you can see?"

"I think I broke my damn toe," Mack grunted.

Getting to his feet, Toshiro trekked inside the penthouse, leaving a trail of chocolate mousse in his wake. He flipped on the lights that Mack had turned off. His husband lay on the floor near the solid wooden leg of a table.

"Did you actually break it?" Toshiro squatted down beside him and reached out to gingerly take his husband's foot in his hand. He gently tested the toe that Mack pointed out to him. "Not sure it's broken, but I've no doubts it'll be sore for a few days at the very least."

Mack dragged a finger through the chocolate on Toshiro's chest, licking his finger clean. "Help me up?"

Toshiro offered a hand up to Mack. "Think you're ready to talk about your sight now?"

"Anyone could bump into a table in the pitch dark," Mack argued.

It hadn't been in the pitch dark, which Mack knew.

Toshiro shook his head at his husband sadly. He'd thought they'd really had a breakthrough earlier.

"Tosh…."

"I'm going to rinse myself off—this suddenly feels sticky in an unpleasant way." Toshiro eased around his husband to head through the room towards the en-suite.

Twisting the taps to get the water perfect, Toshiro stepped underneath the steady stream to wash away his frustration and the mess of pudding on his abdomen. He rested his palms against the cold tiles, dropping his head down. His water-slicked hair covered his face along with the tears that had escaped.

They'd had such an honest moment together on the street. Toshiro hadn't expected his husband to immediately revert back to brushing things aside. He was so lost in his thoughts that he jumped when strong arms wrapped around him from behind.

"It was only a joke, Tosh." Mack rested his face against Toshiro's neck. His trimmed beard rubbed against the sensitive skin, making him shiver slightly. "Not sliding back into denial. I'm sorry I've pushed it away for so long that you've carried such a weight of stress."

"You should be." Toshiro twisted around to face his husband. "We'll do mousse tomorrow."

"Okay then." Mack draped his arms across Toshiro's shoulders. "Shower, then a cuddle while we watch a movie?"

"Brilliant."

The shower ended quickly. Mack tried to make it up to him by gently taking care of him. Toshiro enjoyed the calloused fingers slicked with soap moving across his body.

Once dried off, they ordered up a bottle of wine with a few nibbles to indulge themselves. Toshiro couldn't help laughing when Mack wandered over to let the butler in with a sheet wrapped around his body like a toga. The hotel staff didn't even blink an eye at their antics, which only made him want to know what the man had seen in his time working at Claridge's.

When they'd read the penthouse came with a butler, it had taken everything Toshiro had to rein in Mack's desire to play it up. They had rules about not being dickheads to people just doing their jobs. They had enjoyed the lovely man who told them amazing stories of his time at the hotel.

Their butler had also brought up a selection of DVDs for them. Mack immediately grabbed *Ocean's Eleven*, ignoring Toshiro's groan to pop it into the player. He loved to watch the films and critique all the flaws in the thieves' plans.

"What are the chances we can watch this without you pausing it to rant every five seconds?" Toshiro grabbed one of the chips that they'd ordered from the late night menu.

"Slim to none."

CHAPTER FIFTEEN

MACK

"One does enjoy a day of shopping, doesn't one?"

Mack twisted his head around to the side to avoid busting out into laughter. "Yes, of course."

Punishment.

This has to be punishment.

For some completely unknown reason, Toshiro had transformed himself into the Japanese-British male version of Hyacinth Bucket. Mack's ribs hurt from holding in his laughter. He couldn't get his husband to stop either.

"Oh, *Gregor*, you must see this table. It's simply divine." Toshiro continued on in his overly camp tone, looping his arm around Mack's to guide him towards a different part of the antique market. He bent his head closer to keep from being overheard. "Check out the dealer across the way. The one with the jade figurines."

Leaving Toshiro to distract the dealer, Mack stepped into the narrow stall that made up the antique shop.

He immediately realised what had caught his husband's attention. In the furthest corner of the cramped booth, a locked glass case held rows of coins, several books, and an assortment of other items.

Each one ticked off a box on their list of stolen antiquities, or at the very least, they were amazing fakes. Mack wanted a closer look at them but didn't want to draw attention to them either. They'd already spent longer than intended in the corridor.

Grays seemed more a labyrinth of hallways with antiques than anything else. Mack had sneezed his way through one stall after another. He cleared his throat, tapping his fingers against the side of his leg to draw Toshiro's attention.

They crowded together while pretending to be fascinated by one of the many rugs hanging along the wall. Mack discretely snapped a series of photos with his phone. He made sure to get close-ups of the lock on the cabinet as well as the other security measures within the stall.

They'd already gotten an in-depth look at the CCTV cameras and security system of the building itself. It might've been around for ages, but the owners had definitely updated things.

"Oh, this is simply divine. Isn't it, darling?" Toshiro ran his fingers carefully along a tapestry. "Wouldn't it be perfect in the library over the fireplace?"

"It would." Mack managed to get the words out—barely. He bit the inside of his cheek to attempt to stem back the tide of laughter in him. "Did you see the book? Our collection could certainly stand another addition."

With exaggerated cooing at each other, the two men managed to make their way out of the antique market without drawing the wrong sort of attention to themselves. They'd wanted people to remember their antics, not what they were interested in. He thought Toshiro *Bucket* did the job marvellously.

The second they entered the privacy of their hotel suite, Mack collapsed on the ground in a fit of laughter. He managed after several agonising minutes to restrain himself to a few random chuckles. Toshiro leaned against the wall by the entrance to watch him.

"Is one amused?"

"Oh, fuck. Stop it." Mack rolled onto his back and wiped the tears out of his eyes. "How the hell did you keep a straight face? I think I bit through my cheek to avoid giving us away."

Toshiro smirked down at him. "Amateur."

Mack kicked his husband in the leg. "Arse."

"Are you going to flop around on the floor all afternoon? We've got photos to send to Jude and a bracelet theft to plan. Why you two idiots are so insistent on stealing from Shipton, I'll never understand." Toshiro stepped over Mack, who caught him around the ankle to hold him in place. "Congratulations. You've captured your husband. Care to let me go so I can get your photos uploaded?"

"Already texted them over to Jude." Mack waved his mobile at Toshiro before releasing his ankle. He got to his feet to follow his husband through the small living room into the bedroom. "Dom messaged me while we were pretending to shop. They've got the perfect outfits for our walk in the park."

"And we're certain Shipton goes for a run at the same time every day?" Toshiro had obviously given up on trying to talk him out of the idea. "Won't it stand out that you're suddenly there?"

"Two strangers in a busy park? Doubtful." Mack ignored the tiny sliver of doubt in his mind. "It'll be perfection."

It had to be. Mack knew he'd never live it down if it went as dreadfully wrong as Toshiro quite clearly believed it would go. He, at least, had Jude on his side.

Toshiro eyed him over the top of his laptop. "And don't even think about bringing Jude into this. Neither of you has the best track record when it comes to avoiding questionably risky heists."

"One time. One bloody time and you're always throwing it my face." Mack folded his arms stubbornly across his chest.

"Three times you've actually told me about. Six times if you count the times Jude's admitted to after one too many pints." Toshiro threw one of the decorative pillows from the bed at him. "Never mind the one you dragged Dom into last year."

"One time," Mack insisted. He didn't actually recall the other ones, so they clearly didn't count. "Dom and Jude lie."

"Not usually, and not to me after a beer." Toshiro ducked when Mack flung the pillow back at him. "Want to see what Jude has to say about the photos?"

"I'm sure it's along the lines of us needing to wait a few

weeks, so our faces no longer stand out to the dealers before we attempt to steal anything." Mack already knew exactly what Jude would think. He'd want to join them, using his wheelchair to their advantage. "I'd wager he wants to take part in the actual heist."

"Ding, ding, ding, we have a winner." Toshiro chuckled. "Consider the nonsense in the park as a preview of how we can bring him into future jobs."

Falling back onto the bed, Mack stared up at the ceiling. He'd known Jude eventually would tire of playing the hacker in the shadows. Being in a wheelchair hadn't changed who their friend was at his core.

Of the group, Jude had always been the most active next to Mack. His friend managed to combine brute force with his skills with breaking into any electronic system. His level of anticipation grew for getting one over on Shipton.

Was it petty?

Probably.

She brought out the worst in him. A fact Mack tried to forget. As Jude would say, his skills at living in denial were unmatched.

It'll be brilliant. We'll get the bauble off her wrist, and have a pint to celebrate. Jude'll get his thieving mojo back.

It'll be brilliant.

CHAPTER SIXTEEN

TOSHIRO

"It was weird."

"It was." Mack twisted the delicate bracelet encrusted with a massive number of diamonds in his hand. "Too easy."

Toshiro took the bracelet from his husband before he broke it with his twirling. "What do we always say about a heist that's far too easy?"

Mack flipped him off without giving him a verbal response. Toshiro found it amusing. He didn't really need words to know what his husband was thinking.

The adventure in the park had gone far too smoothly for either of their liking. Their target, the petulant Mary Shipton, had been utterly unaware of her surroundings. Jude had easily been able to slip the bracelet from her wrist while Mack pushed him around the park in his wheelchair.

No thief is that unaware of the people around them.
And if they are, they get locked up.

Toshiro touched a finger to the bracelet before holding it

up to the morning light shining through the window. "What do they gain from allowing us to steal this?"

"Nothing?"

His husband shrugged before heading into the kitchen to grab the kettle whistling on the hob. Toshiro returned the bracelet to one of the three hidden safes in their loft and followed him in to get a top-up on his tea. He didn't believe in coincidences, not when it came to jewellery worth millions.

But what do Rafe and Mary gain from it?

No matter what Mack thought, Toshiro had no doubt Rafe had a finger in the situation if his protégé was involved. The man had always been a control freak. It had been partly what led to the rift between them.

My Gregor has always been a wild thing.

With fresh tea in hand, Toshiro enjoyed the pleasure of watching his husband cooking for him. They'd gotten up before dawn, as their target jogged in the park early in the morning. It had all be over and done within thirty minutes.

And I still find it odd.

"You're obsessing." Mack casually flipped an egg in the pan, cheering when it landed perfectly. "I am the king of breakfast."

"Are we just going to ignore the twenty eggs you've flung all over the kitchen while practising?" Toshiro smirked at him and then saluted him with his cup. "I distinctly recall you picking scrambled eggs out of your hair yesterday."

"Where's the love and unconditional support of my beloved husband?"

"I unconditionally support you not getting my breakfast in your hair." Toshiro enjoyed the smell of bacon getting crisp. "And I'm not obsessing."

Maybe a little.

Oddities during a theft always bothered Toshiro. He disliked not having enough insight into the situation. Was it merely odd—or a broader conspiracy?

Toshiro knew Rafe couldn't be trusted. And if Mary Shipton had completely bought into him as a mentor, neither could she. The old bastard didn't suffer fools, so she had to be a capable thief.

Capable enough to see through the simplest of tricks.

Placing his cup to one side, Toshiro left the kitchen to hunt for his phone. Jude and Mack weren't the most objective, so he decided to reach out to Dom and Charlie. His twin, in particular, often had insights into a situation that a non-autistic tended to miss.

Toshiro: Thoughts on the great bracelet caper?

Dom: Charlie thinks it's bullshit.

Dom: Sorry. Charlie isn't as uncouth as I am. I think it's bullshit. She says it's highly suspicious.

Toshiro: Agreed. But why? What would she gain from allowing the theft?

Dom: No fucking clue. I'll ask my smarter half.

Dom: Charlie thinks it's a two-part con. Lull us into believing she's not as savvy, then hit us with whatever she and Rafe have been planning.

Toshiro: But why?

Dom: She doesn't have any idea. Neither do I.

What does Mack say?

Toshiro: I'm obsessing.

Dom: He has a blind spot when it comes to Rafe.

Dom: No pun intended.

Toshiro: You two coming over later to talk about the antique market? Or are we meeting up at Jude's this time?

Dom: Jude's.

"Quit gossiping about me and come have breakfast." Mack snatched the phone out of his hands. "What's the consensus?"

"You're daft."

"Aside from the obvious?" Mack tossed the phone in the general direction of the counter and grabbed Toshiro by the shoulder to drag him into the kitchen. "I don't see the point of worrying about it."

Neither did your dad, and he's in prison.

Leaving the thought unspoken, Toshiro decided to keep his concerns to himself. He'd watch carefully for any signs of actions from either Rafe or his young protégé. There honestly wasn't much else to be done.

His only other option would be to see what the authorities had on Mary Shipton. Why had she come out of nowhere to insinuate herself as she had into their circle of acquaintances? Coincidences rarely happened so frequently involving the same person.

What motivates a person, outside of just money?

"What do we know about her family? Aside from the

obvious similar links to piracy between the Eastons and Shiptons." Toshiro couldn't stop himself from asking the question.

"Mary's?"

Toshiro nodded. He accepted the plate from Mack who joined him at the small table in their kitchen. "Where'd she come from? How did she even know about Rafe? Aside from his reputation, he's not the easiest man to find to simply walk up to. He's made a career of being a chameleon that slinks in and out of society without anyone even realising who he is. He's got more passports than both of us put together. As far as I know, none of her immediate family have been in the business. Not in the last century or more. Why now? Why her?"

"All good questions. Why did Rafe even accept her? He swore off working with a partner after we fought. And now we're both obsessing." Mack nudged him in the calf with his bare foot. "I made your breakfast in my boxers. Shouldn't you show more appreciation?"

"I'll show you appreciation after I've had breakfast." Toshiro shovelled bacon into his mouth. They'd been up at five in the morning and not bothered to take the time to eat. "Are you going to play footsie or eat your brekkie?"

"I can multitask." Mack pointed his toast at Toshiro when he went to reply. "Now is not the time to provide all your many examples to the contrary. Just accept I can feel you up and scarf down eggs and bacon without skipping a beat."

"Sure. I'll be sure to mark the momentous occasion of

you being able to multitask, but maybe when you're not dribbling marmalade down your beard." He snickered when Mack immediately dropped his toast to swipe at his beard. "*Kidding.*"

"Lick it off?"

"And get hair in my teeth?"

They froze for a second before giggling like two schoolchildren. Toshiro grabbed a nearby kitchen towel to toss over to Mack. The strange mood that had lingered between them lifted with their laughter.

"I sent an email to my doctor."

Toshiro choked on his sip of tea, almost snorting it painfully through his nose. "And?"

"Got an appointment for two weeks from now. The doctor is apparently on vacation until then." Mack balled up the towel in his hands. "Go with me?"

"Where else would I be but at your side?" Toshiro shifted his chair around to sit next to his husband. He covered Mack's fidgeting fingers with his own. "Whatever happens, Gregor, we'll handle it."

CHAPTER SEVENTEEN

MACK

Distraction, Mack found, didn't come nearly as smoothly as hoped. The wait for his appointment made it seem as if everything around him went in slow motion. He wanted it over—to hear the worst and be done with it.

Even the Mary mystery didn't do anything to drag his mind away from the growing fear. Mack tried to think logically about it. He told himself aside from the night blindness, his sight hadn't gotten drastically worse since his last visit to the doctor however many years ago it was.

None of it worked.

Anxiety gnawed at his usually confident exterior. Mack found it impossible to focus on anything important. He'd missed several meetings, and even forgotten to do surveillance on the antique market.

Now sitting at the office waiting to be seen, Mack shifted around in the seat next to Toshiro. His foot tapped incessantly against the floor while he absently bit at his thumbnail. All signs of his usually calm nature had flown out the window.

What is she going to say?

Am I finally going to be declared legally blind?

The question bounced around his mind like a ricocheting bullet, making it even harder for him to control his nerves. Toshiro rested his hand on Mack's knee to squeeze it gently. He was grateful his husband didn't offer any platitudes to assuage his anxiety.

Mack hadn't felt this tense since they'd waltzed into an embassy to retrieve a lost painting for the family of a holocaust survivor. He still didn't know how they'd pulled the job off. The tears in the son's eyes had made it worth it.

"Mr Ueda-Easton?"

Mack wanted to ignore the nurse even as his husband gave his knee an encouraging squeeze. "Not sure my legs will hold me."

"They will." Toshiro stood up and waited patiently with his hand out towards him. "You can do this. You made the appointment, drove us here, made it through the front door, and didn't moan too much about the tests the nurse put you through. The hard part is done; all you have to do is get to your feet."

"That's all, is it?" Mack thought it sounded a great deal harder than his husband claimed. He stared at the hand for several seconds before grabbing it. "Into the breach?"

"Into the breach." Toshiro waited for him to stand before he gave him a quick hug. "We'll manage; whatever she tells us, we'll figure it out."

The nurse stayed discreetly quiet until Mack shook

himself out of the fear that froze him in place. He gave Toshiro's hand a grateful squeeze and walked confidently towards the open door. The time had come to stop pretending his vision wasn't progressively getting worse.

"Dr Smith will be just a moment. She's checking out the scans of your eyes we took when you arrived." The nurse led them to one of the open rooms and motioned for them to step inside. "If you need anything in the meantime, I'll be right outside."

"Thank you." Toshiro spoke when it became clear Mack had lost his battle with nerves on seeing the examination room. "Gregor?"

Mack shook his head when his husband tried to offer words of comfort to him in French—one of the few languages they had in common. "Why do you always fall into another language?"

"Charlie says the translator portion of my brain got jumbled, and I forget which one to use." Toshiro shrugged. He wrapped his arms around Mack. "It's hard to face your fears."

"Is that what I'm doing?" Mack soaked in the comfort from his husband. He appreciated Toshiro being there for him as he always was. "Facing my fears? Not sure I'm actually dealing with it."

"You're here. You didn't bolt for the door." Toshiro tightened his hold on him. "And don't even think about trying it now for shits and giggles."

Mack clutched his hand to his chest and gave an affronted gasp. "I would never."

"*Liar.*" Toshiro snickered at him.

Mack joined him laughing when his husband muttered in Portuguese at him for almost two full minutes. "I've no sodding clue what you said so I'll assume you told me how much you love and admire me."

"Fair enough."

"You two gents decent?" Dr Deborah Smith tapped on the door before stepping inside with a chart and tablet in her hand. "Well, Mr—"

"Save yourself time and call me Gregor." Mack cut her off before he spent the entire visit having to listen to "Ueda-Easton." Toshiro elbowed him in the side, probably for rudely interrupting the doctor. "Sorry."

She waved his apology off, dragging a wheeled chair over to sit in front of them. "I'm pleased you've come in to see me. I worried you'd stay away as some patients do."

Ten minutes into the visit, Mack started to tune her out. Dr Smith was clearly passionate about all the latest treatments and research being done. He really wanted to tell her to get on with it.

If the worst was happening, Mack didn't see the point in dragging it all out. *Am I fucking going to be blind by the end of the year?* A sharp elbow in the side told him that he'd said that out loud.

Bugger.

"I'm so sorry." Mack thought from her muffled giggling that she found his outburst less horrifying than his husband had. Toshiro glared at him stonily. "I said sorry."

The doctor wisely decided to halt her spiel and get to

the point. His night vision, in particular, had progressed as they'd warned him. *No bloody shit.* She offered a life raft to him in the form of confirming his sight hadn't deteriorated much beyond it.

She'd tested his peripheral vision and been pleased to see it hadn't started to tunnel down. On the whole, he'd been one of the lucky ones, though she cautioned him on pushing himself. It would progress eventually.

He left with a sheet of supplements to try out. The doctor had advised how researchers found a regimen of vitamins and Omega-3s had the potential to slow vision loss. He didn't see any harm in giving it a try; it was less invasive and scary than many of the other clinical trials being done.

Stepping outside after the visit was finished, Mack almost raced to get out to the car park. He irrationally feared they'd call him back to say it was a mistake, and he'd be declared legally blind now. Toshiro seemed to understand—thankfully—moving to handle wrapping up the paperwork for him.

Crouching by the car, Mack rested his head on the bonnet. He breathed in and out deeply until the faint feeling disappeared. The worst hadn't happened, and he struggled to process all of it.

"Right. So eat more fish—eat healthier. Take supplements. Keep wearing your sunglasses during the day, and no driving at night." Toshiro leaned against the Fiat 500 they'd *borrowed* for the week. "Can you manage not greasing up your diet for a bit?"

"I eat fish." Mack scrunched himself into the car. He'd been amazed at how spacious it was for a small vehicle, but his six-foot frame still felt cramped. "What? I do."

"Fish and chips don't count." Toshiro clambered into the Fiat, banging his knees against the dashboard.

"It's fish."

"Battered and fried. I'm fairly confident that's not what Dr Smith had in mind." Toshiro fought with his seat belt until it released enough for him to get it on correctly. "I'll sort out the supplements. A change in our eating won't kill either of us."

"Might," Mack grumbled. "I'm not giving up steak—or biscuits."

CHAPTER EIGHTEEN

TOSHIRO

"Tosh? You here? Mack said to head up." Charlie skipped into the living room with a paper bag in hand. "Want a scone? Mum made them."

Toshiro held his hand up without even glancing away from his laptop. He'd missed a deadline for the online magazine that paid him to write travel articles. "How's tricks?"

"Dom and Jude are trying to convince Mack the feeble old man con would work brilliantly with the dealer. It won't. Jude broke his wheelchair trying to make it go faster. Dom's mad at him because in the process he rode right over one of her new statues. Mary Shipton flew out to Dubai this morning. Rafe went to Istanbul. I ate three scones." Charlie climbed up on the sofa to sit on the arm with her shoes on the cushion. "Oh, and Mum wants to go on vacation in September."

Toshiro paused mid-thought to process all of the information his sister dumped on him. "Why do I suddenly feel a sense of dread about this vacation plan?"

"Mum wants us *all* to go to Japan for *Shūbun no Hi.*" Charlie opened the bag to grab one of the scones, holding it out for him to get one for himself. "It's on the autumnal equinox. We haven't been in a while."

The Japanese held a festival during the equinox to honour their ancestors. Toshiro knew their mother had her own way of remembering their lost relatives each September. They hadn't been to her home since the few remaining members of his mum's family had died tragically when a tsunami hit the country.

Their mum's heart had been broken. She hadn't made her annual trip to Japan since. Toshiro saved the document he'd been writing in to pull up a calendar. *Am I a terrible son if I claim sudden plague to avoid this? Yes, yes I am.*

"We've got a few months to plan it out." Charlie craned her head around to get a peek at the calendar. She snagged yet another scone from the bag. "How'd it go with Dr Debbie?"

"Dr *Smith.*" Toshiro glared at his giggling sister, who'd latched on to the name of Mack's physician and found it hilarious for some unknown reason. She had a tendency to find amusement out of the way words sounded together. "It went brilliantly. Better than expected."

"Mack seemed a bit unhappy. I think. I can't always tell when he's being quiet or when he's upset." Charlie tucked her legs up more. "Is his sight worse?"

"He's a whiny prat because I'm making him eat better." Toshiro had taken the notes from the doctor seriously. Their diet had completely changed in the last few days. He'd even gone so far as to empty out their fridge and cupboards, giving the food to a family a few streets away who struggled to make do. "You'd think salad came with a side of arsenic."

"But is his sight worse?" Charlie folded and unfolded the top of the paper bag repeatedly.

Toshiro grabbed one of the fidget cubes he kept around the house for when his sister visited and held it out for her. She immediately pressed the little buttons on one side of the stim toy. "His sight hasn't gotten much worse. We knew he had problems at night, but *Dr Debbie* was pleased with how he's doing. With any luck, Mack will go many years before he's hit with any seriously drastic changes."

"So, good?"

"Good."

"Then why's he sad?" Charlie twisted the cube around to find the silver ball bearing on one of the sides, spinning it with her thumb. "Or upset."

"Because he hates eating healthy."

"But if it's to help him, why would it make him upset?" Charlie asked, sounding completely bewildered.

Toshiro scratched his head for a second trying to decide the easiest way to explain it to his twin. "Sometimes, non-autistics aren't logical."

"Scone?" She held out the bag to him. "Last one."

Splitting the scone in half so Charlie could have some, Toshiro asked her about the dangerous duo travelling overseas. Jude had been monitoring Rafe's movements for years. He trusted the man about as much as Toshiro did.

So not even a little.

Curious how easy it's been to keep track of the elusive man.

A tad too curious, actually.

"Tosh?" Charlie nudged him with the tip of her trainer. "What's wrong? You've gone all weird thinky face."

He chuckled at her for a second. Charlie had always referred to any expression of his that she didn't understand as his "thinky" face. "Do you find it strange we so easily discovered where Mary and Rafe were travelling?"

Charlie stared down at her cube while considering his question. "Maybe. We never travel under our actual names unless we're with Mum. Why would they? He's been doing this longer than all of us."

"And once again, I'm wondering why?" Toshiro knew discussing anything Rafe-related would upset Mack. His husband continued to stubbornly ignore the obvious signs around his mentor. "Is this even directed at us, or are we simply observant bystanders caught up by coincidence?"

"You don't believe in coincidences." Charlie dropped the cube on the cushion next to her. "Neither do I. There's got to be CCTV footage that Jude can get access to. Maybe we can see if they even arrived in the cities they purchased tickets for?"

"Does Mum still have the friend who travels to Dubai for vacations?" Toshiro tried to avoid talking to their mother about her friends. They all tended to be women with expensive tastes who hit on him, even after learning about his husband. *Creepy.* "The one with the diplomat for a husband? He worked at the embassy over there. I wonder if we could get an invite to visit."

While Charlie wandered into the kitchen to grab a drink, Toshiro returned to his laptop. *Two talented thieves heading to countries near the areas we know antiquities are being stolen from? What are the odds they're involved in all of this?*

Toshiro considered sending a text to Pierce, then changed his mind. He trusted Mack's uncle, but it didn't seem fair to put the man in an awkward position. They'd find another way to get the information he wanted without his husband being aware at all.

"Tosh?"

He found his sister holding a packet of biscuits. "Where'd you find them?"

"Top shelf of the cabinet near the fridge behind your old tea set." Charlie made her inspection of his kitchen sound completely normal. "I can't find my cup."

His twin tended to stress out if she couldn't use the same utensils outside of her flat. She had everything set up at her place perfectly, but everywhere else occasionally caused her anxiety. Toshiro had learned over the years to work around it.

If Charlie needed him to keep one set of dishes just for her, Toshiro would do it without complaint. He refused to be one more person in his twin's life who forced her out of her comfort zone simply because they couldn't be bothered to step outside of their non-autistic world. His sister never asked him to do it.

"Mum reorganised the last time she visited. I did manage to convince her one cabinet was for your stuff. It's the middle one over the toaster." Toshiro placed his laptop on the sofa and joined her in the kitchen. "You know how she *loves* to make things easier for us."

"Mum thinks easier means harder." Charlie hopped up and down when she found the cabinet contained several identical Peter Rabbit mugs.

"Mack worried yours might break, so he bought several more."

The mugs were old; in fact, the original had been the only gift left from their father. Charlie's first one had broken when their cat knocked it off a counter. Mack had hunted down as many as he could find online for her.

They'd decided not to surprise her with them as a wrapped present. Charlie hated attention. On birthdays, she usually grabbed all her gifts to open them in private without anyone watching. He'd been waiting for her to find the mugs.

Mack had also gotten her a Peter Rabbit egg cup, which she appeared to be clutching to her chest like the most precious thing in the world. Toshiro wished he'd had a camera going so Mack could see how happy it had made her. He loved how thoughtful his cheeky husband was.

"Still want tea?" Toshiro grabbed the kettle to fill it with water. "So, genius twin of mine, how should I proceed with the Rafe and Mary situation?"

While making her favourite herbal tea blend, Toshiro brainstormed with his twin. She had a fantastic ability to see problems from perspectives he'd never even considered. It often wound up being the difference between success and failure.

In the end, Toshiro had to acknowledge he ran the risk of spreading himself far too thin to handle everything. A distracted thief tended to be a locked up thief. His twin suggested waiting until they'd finished following the path the villa documents had led them down.

"You never know, Tosh. They might be connected." Charlie glanced towards the door when it opened. "Dommy."

They might be connected.

No, could they be?

Shit.

CHAPTER NINETEEN

MACK

"Gregor."

Mack managed to keep from tripping over his feet when a familiar figure joined him on the park path. He continued on his jog, forcing his uncle to fall in step with him. "Should I expect to be grabbed and thrown in the back of one of Interpol's blacked-out SUVs?"

"You? Not yet. Me? Maybe."

Mack did stumble over a crack in the pavement then. He caught himself and slowed down to allow for more relaxed conversation. "What the hell are you talking about? You're the cleanest damn officer I've ever seen, which is strange considering our illustrious family history. What would you possibly get pinched for?"

Pierce breathed out a heavy sigh that made Mack feel sorry enough to stop teasing. His uncle waited until they'd passed a few other early morning joggers to continue. "There are six people in my department. One of them has been falsifying incoming reports of stolen items from other offices. Don't know which one it is."

Mack came to a stop and stretched his leg out on a nearby bench. "Why tell me about it? I'm not exactly in the business of helping the police—and they certainly aren't going to use me as a character witness."

"I didn't track you down in the morning to enjoy the pleasure of your jokes." Pierce continued to scowl at Mack but shook his head when Mack wasn't fazed by him. "This isn't a joke, Gregor. I'm about to lose not only my career but my freedom as well. My reputation will be ripped to shreds. I've worked damn hard to step out of the tarnish of the family name."

"And what? I'm no superhero."

"I know you're trying to track down the thieves behind the stolen antiquities. It's bigger than just them." Pierce lowered his voice even further forcing Mack to lean in closer to hear. "Family's important."

"It is." Mack frowned in confusion at his uncle who simply shook his hand. "What—"

His uncle spun on his heel and strode quickly away from him. Mack stared blankly at Pierce until he'd disappeared. He switched his attention to the key resting in the palm of his hand.

Curious.

What the hell kind of rabbit hole are we all about to fall into now?

Mack immediately recognised the key as one belonging to a safe deposit box. His phone beeped seconds later with a curious scramble of letters. He scratched his beard absently, trying to decipher it.

On the brink of giving up, Mack remembered his dad mentioning how his mum and her brother had loved to send coded messages to one another to hide from their parents. He had several of her journals at home in their safe. With any luck, one would contain the cypher key to unlocking the message.

And the safe deposit box.

Toshiro pounced on him the minute Mack stepped into the loft ten minutes later. "*Merde*. Your uncle was arrested by Interpol. They're keeping it hush-hush. He's being taken out of the country for questioning."

"Shit. Already? How'd you find out?" Mack dashed by Toshiro, who followed him over to the safe.

"Dom."

Mack knew Dom kept her family connections for just such purposes. "Hold this key for a minute, will you?"

Ignoring the confusion on his husband's face, Mack quickly eased the section of wooden flooring up to reveal the smallest of their hidden safes. He pressed his thumb against the biometric lock, waiting impatiently for it to open. Toshiro seemed to grow even more bewildered when Mack came out with the journals.

"How exactly are your mum's teenage diaries going to help?" Toshiro joined him on the sofa where Mack handed him half of the stack of notebooks. "What are we looking for?"

"Anything to do with the special code my uncle and

mum created. I've got a message to decipher, but no sodding clue how to do it." Mack hadn't expected Interpol to move as quickly as they had. He wondered who on his uncle's team had gotten their hands dirty enough to need to use Pierce as a scapegoat. "Bloody hell, my mum was angst-filled in her teens."

"Want to hear about her first kiss?" Toshiro grinned at him.

"No." Mack shuddered then smacked his husband on the leg with one of the books. "Focus. Fuck. This is pointless."

"Patience, *amor.*"

"Show off." Mack rolled his eyes when Toshiro decided to actually show off by rattling off in several different languages. "No clue what you said."

"Good."

They elbowed each other a few times until Mack called *pax.* Thirty minutes of muttering over the journals had him ready to throw in the towel. Toshiro dropped one of the diaries over the one that Mack had been perusing.

Amidst whining about his father, who his mum had apparently just begun to date, Mack found an oddly grouped section of letters. He realised it was exactly what he'd been searching for. They managed to quickly put together the code to the corresponding alphabet.

He deciphered the note from his uncle quickly—*Metropolitan Safe Deposits. Knightsbridge. 11049.* "Well? Fancy a trip across town?"

"Of course." Toshiro had already gathered up the journals to replace them in the safe. "It's like our very own mystery.

Are we in *The Da Vinci Code?* You're Tom Hanks."

"And you're an idiot."

After taking a quick shower to wash off his jog sweat, Mack changed into a nondescript grey T-shirt and jeans. They picked up Nico on the way. He had no direct connection to Pierce so they hoped it wouldn't raise any suspicions.

"And you don't think the lovely people at Metropolitan won't find it strange that I'm opening Pierce's safe?" Nico sat forward in their BMW; Mack had traded in the Fiat the previous day. His head poked between the two front seats. "I mean, I'm not the sort Pierce Siddall hangs out with."

Mack held the key out to him. "Please?"

"Only because you asked nicely." Nico smirked.

"Prat." Mack flicked the key to Nico who slid out of the door. "He really is a cheeky sod."

"Helping him was the best decision we ever made." Toshiro smiled fondly.

"Marrying you was the best decision I ever made." Mack would never regret giving Nico the much-needed hand up. "He might be a close second, though. Kid's done well for himself."

"And us."

Time ticked away slowly. Mack glanced around periodically to ensure no one snuck up on them. With all the CCTV, they couldn't exactly avoid being seen entirely if anyone happened to be watching.

"Should we go in?" Toshiro glanced at his watch, his phone, and then the clock in the car.

"No. But you can check my watch as well if you like,"

Mack teased him. "Here's my phone too. Fairly confident they all say the same time."

Leaving his husband to curse him out in Japanese, Mack put the car into gear in preparation of Nico's arrival. The young fence slipped into the back seat seconds later. He pulled away from the kerb to blend into London traffic.

Nico shifted over to the middle of the back seat, easing forward again to push two large manila envelopes over to Toshiro. "I waited until no one else was in the room to open it up. The box only had these two in it. One's got your name on it, Mack-n-cheese."

"You're not funny." Mack flipped him off.

"Toto thinks I'm funny."

Mack grinned at his husband, who had stopped laughing to curse Nico out. "Apparently, he doesn't think you're funny."

"I could've been at home in my pyjamas eating dry Weetabix with Nutella while watching *This Morning* on the telly. Instead, I got dressed and dragged my arse out to do you two a favour. The least you can do is find me funny." Nico twisted around to stretch out on the back seat. "Wake me up when you've gotten to my flat, Mack-n-cheese."

"Kids these days." Toshiro pulled off his jacket and draped it across the already snoring Nico. He'd learned early on how to fall asleep quickly but lightly, a painful reminder of his time living on the street. "Think we should wait until we're at home to open this."

"Agreed."

They stayed at Nico's for an hour, ensuring he ate

something other than Weetabix. Mack finally had to drag Toshiro away. His husband had quickly fallen into an argument with the younger man about which doctor from the *Doctor Who* series was the best one.

They're both wrong.

Tennant's clearly the most brilliant.

Nerds.

The envelopes taunted Mack the entire ride back to their loft. His curiosity ate at his patience. It didn't help that Toshiro had put in one of his CDs of French pop music and started to sing along to it, loudly and badly.

His husband had many talents. Singing definitely wasn't one of them. Mack didn't want to risk Toshiro's wrath by turning it off.

He'd made the mistake once, and slept on the sofa for a week.

To the relief of his ears and his patience, they avoided spots of bad traffic to arrive quickly at the loft. Mack parked speedily and raced through his offices upstairs to their place. He'd already gotten the envelopes open when Toshiro caught up with him.

"Well?"

"It's not the location of the holy grail." Mack had placed the contents in two different stacks. He flipped through the first. "Where are the documents we found at the villa, Toshi?"

"Hang on." Toshiro grabbed them from the desk across the room. "Here. What'd you find?"

"Files. I think these are Pierce's files on the antiquities thefts." Mack grabbed one of the sheets of paper to hold it up side by side to the translation of what they'd found in Italy. "Take a look at these together."

"The objects are the same. Dates and locations are all wrong." Toshiro bent over the back of the sofa to read them better. He pointed his finger at something towards the bottom of Pierce's version. "I'd say your uncle copied down a report from whoever has framed him that was used to falsify when the items went missing. If the authorities search in the wrong city and go through CCTV for different dates, they'd never catch the criminals in action."

"We're criminals."

"*Technically.*"

CHAPTER TWENTY

TOSHIRO

"Can I help you?" Toshiro glanced at the smartly dressed woman who'd taken the seat across from him at the table. She'd apparently bided her time until Mack went to the loo. "Whatever you're selling, I'm definitely not interested."

"Seeta Joseph."

"Still not interested." Toshiro looked towards the hall where Mack had disappeared. *What the hell is keeping him?* "I've no idea who you are."

Ms Joseph held out her warrant card identifying her as a detective sergeant. "You're a difficult couple to find."

"Yet, you managed it and conveniently waited until my husband had left the table to approach." Toshiro kept his cool, mentally repeating the information on her badge so Jude could do a bit of research on her. "Why exactly are you hunting for us?"

"Pierce Siddall."

"What about him?" Toshiro hated playing twenty

questions, particularly with a plainclothes detective from the Metropolitan police.

"We've worked together for months on a case, but suddenly it's been taken away from me. I'm told to move on to other cases. They claim Pierce is crooked." She frowned at Toshiro with her fingers clutched around the wallet containing her identification. "Pierce Siddall would sooner take a leap off Big Ben than throw his career away for a few quid."

"I'm sure it's more than a few quid." Mack stepped up behind him, placing his hands on Toshiro's shoulders. His husband's attention was laser-focused on the British Indian woman across the table. "I'm not exactly inclined to trust the police right now."

"Neither am I, and I am one." She shoved her wallet back into her jacket pocket. "If they've sunk Pierce, I've no doubts I'll be next."

Ahh, self-interest, now that I definitely believe.

Toshiro reached up to squeeze Mack's hand to silence him. "What do you believe we can accomplish that you can't?"

"Not a bloody thing." She seemed affronted that he'd even suggested it. "Look, I'm not even sure why I'm here. Working with criminals won't exactly provide me with evidence I can use to convince my superiors to free Pierce."

"We're *definitely* not sure why you're here." Mack crossed his arms and completely ignored the warning glare from Toshiro. "Or, why you think we're not the most upstanding of citizens? I'm insulted."

"Pierce." She held her hand up to stop Mack from retorting. "He was desperate at the time." Elbowing his husband in the stomach, Toshiro tried to soothe the situation. He had a feeling Pierce had left their information with her. The man had to have some sort of failsafe other than the files they'd collected.

If they intended to put all the puzzle pieces together, Toshiro knew they'd require cooperation from the detective sergeant. Antagonising her wouldn't serve any purpose whatsoever. Mack flicked him on the back of the head but thankfully stayed silent.

"What are you expecting from us?" Toshiro wanted the detective gone before Mack decided to insert himself into the conversation again. "The police don't generally come knocking on our door for help."

And if they do come knocking, we're usually out the back door.

"I can handle finding the thieving bastard in my department or Pierce's, but you'll have better luck finding his contacts. The only way to prove Pierce innocent is to either find concrete evidence or catch them in the act." She dropped her eyes to the papers on the table and smiled when Toshiro calmly flipped them over. Her gaze moved up to Mack. "Don't you want to help your uncle?"

Toshiro reached back to squeeze Mack's leg. "Have a card, Detective Sergeant? We'll think on your offer and let you know."

Tossing her card on the table, the detective disappeared out of the café. Mack flopped dramatically into the chair. He waved the server over to get a top-up of their coffees.

Toshiro snapped a photo of the card and texted it over to Jude. "What the hell have we gotten ourselves involved in this time?"

"Not a clue." Mack grabbed the card from him. "Seeta Joseph. Why's her name so familiar?"

"Is it?" Toshiro didn't remember ever hearing it. He tended to have the better memory for names. Mack usually recalled faces, yet another reason they partnered so well. "Maybe Pierce mentioned her?"

"It'll come to me." Mack pocketed the card. He tapped his finger on the rim of his coffee mug. "Think she meant it?"

"Maybe?" Toshiro shrugged.

Pierce aside, their experiences with the police hadn't been brilliant. *Granted, we are villains in their eyes. Can't say I blame them.* Toshiro didn't know if they could afford to trust her.

"What if she's the one who set Pierce up?"

Toshiro hadn't considered that angle. "And we're what? Another set of stooges for her? Why not just lock us up immediately? Why the ruse of trying to free him?"

"Proper villains like complicated plans." Mack nodded sagely.

"And we're…?"

"Robbing the villains to help their victims," Mack teased.

"You're seriously not allowed to watch *Robin Hood* ever again. Not even the Errol Flynn one." Toshiro smiled at his husband's immediate gasp of outrage. "What? You get all vigilante when you feel as if you've a kindred spirit in him."

"I don't."

"You wanted a tattoo of him on your back." Toshiro took great joy in reminding his husband of the time he'd drunkenly attempted to get Robin Hood inked on his entire back. "I believe it was the Russell Crowe version that time?"

"I hate you." Mack flipped him off. "Are you finished with your coffee?"

"Finished?" Toshiro stared down at the mug that had only recently been refilled. "Not even I can drink it that quickly."

"I think we should go to Manchester."

"That's like two hours on a train. Or four if we drive. Is this punishment for mocking you? If I suck your cock, do we still have to go?" Toshiro was opposed to any drive requiring him to sit in a car for over an hour—especially when they'd end up getting stuck in traffic. "Why?"

"Because Pierce's flat and office are in Manchester. We're going to pay Interpol a visit." Mack grinned slightly manically at him.

"You have lost your mind." Toshiro watched as his husband paid the bill, gathered up their stuff, and grabbed his hand to tug him up from his chair. "Really? We're doing this now without any planning?"

"Why not? We haven't had sex on a train in ages." Mack dodged out of the way of his shove. "C'mon, Toshi. Live large with me. I'll get Jude to get the tickets for us. We can stop by the loft to switch out our identities and pack a bag."

Toshiro, as always, found it impossible to resist the

cajoling of his hazel-eyed husband. "We're not going in blind, though. If Detective Joseph isn't responsible, we don't want anyone in Pierce's unit to know we're onto them."

Mack grabbed him by the hand as they made the ten-minute walk back to their loft from the coffee shop. "You're brilliant."

"For stating the obvious?" Toshiro raised an eyebrow at him.

"For marrying me." Mack yanked him into his arms, wrapping his arms tightly around Toshiro. "Actually, maybe it's a sign of your lack of intelligence. You voluntarily connected yourself to me for life."

"Yeah, I buggered things up spectacularly," he chuckled.

"I'll bugger you spectacularly," Mack promised darkly.

CHAPTER TWENTY-ONE

MACK

"No."

"But Toshi."

"No."

"C'mon, Tosh," Mack cajoled.

"We're not nineteen anymore. I'm not screwing around in the bathroom of the train," Toshiro hissed at him, trying to avoid drawing the attention of the other passengers. Even in first class, they were close enough to be potentially overheard. "Let's try not to get arrested before we even get to Manchester, shall we?"

"How about on Pierce's desk?" Mack bent forward to brush his lips against Toshiro's neck, on the spot beneath his ear that always drove him crazy. "Pay him back for all the trouble he's caused us."

"Not sure getting arrested is him causing trouble for us."

"Is that a yes or a no?" Mack nibbled on his husband's earlobe.

After several minutes of travelling in silence, Mack eased his jacket off to drape it across his lap. *Strategically.* He grinned when Toshiro scowled at him. *Time to have a bit of fun to make the hours go by more quickly.*

"What do you think you're doing, Gregor?" Toshiro asked when Mack circled his fingers around his husband's wrist and guided Toshiro's hand underneath the jacket to rest in his lap. "Do you honestly want damp boxers for the whole trip and however long it takes us to get to our hotel? Not sure waltzing around Manchester with cum in your pants is the most brilliant idea you've ever had."

He didn't. While packing for the journey, he'd had the foresight to slip a spare pair of boxers into his pocket. Toshiro, of course, didn't need to know.

After a moment of thought, Toshiro appeared to decide his damp underwear would be well worth the risk of being caught wanking in their first class seats on the train. His husband managed with minimal movement of the jacket to get his hand into Mack's trousers. The searching fingers quickly dipped inside his boxers.

Is there a better way to spend a two-hour journey?

No, there really isn't.

Spreading his legs apart slightly, Mack eased further down in the seat. It allowed both the jacket and the table to provide additional cover. Toshiro's fingers nimbly danced around the head of his cock, slowly edging him into a full erection.

Mack dropped his head against the seat, struggling to keep his breathing level. Toshiro would never let him hear the end of it someone caught them out because of his inability to maintain his composure. *Fuck, it's hard, though.*

Pun intended?

I'm such an idiot.

Well, it wouldn't be the first time we got caught in a compromising position.

A point of pride for both of them was the time they'd snuck into the gallery at the Royal Albert Hall. One of the ushers found them with their trousers down. Mack still didn't know how they'd managed to talk their way out of serious trouble.

Barely catching himself from humping into Toshiro's skilful fingers, Mack almost jumped in his seat a second later when his husband switched up his stroking. The sudden change in pace brought him dangerously close to climax. He steadied his breathing again, turning his head to stare at the passing countryside for a distraction.

It became evident Toshiro wanted to drive him to orgasm quickly. His husband knew every caress guaranteed to make Mack insane. And, as always, it worked like a charm.

Mack dug his nails into the palm of his hand to try to keep himself under control. He'd barely regained his ability to think clearly when one of their fellow passengers came strolling past their seats, stopping to ask if they had the time. "It's about half-past ten, I think."

Toshiro discreetly wiped his fingers on the inside of Mack's boxers and extracted his hand once the passenger continued on their way. "Enjoy your sticky situation."

Giving his husband a wink, Mack got to his feet and

squeezed by him. He quickly made his way to the nearest loo. Swapping his boxers in the cramped space required a bit of contortion, but he managed it.

"Cleaned up?" Toshiro said playfully when Mack returned to his seat.

"Messy boxers aren't conducive to the coolness that is me." Mack blinked in surprise when his husband dropped a phone in his hands. "Problem?"

"Seeta Joseph."

Mack briefly read through the information Jude had texted over on her. "She's a bit squeaky clean."

"A bit too squeaky clean." Toshiro nodded. "Question is, what are we risking by not at least playing along with her for a while? It might lead us closer to getting your uncle free."

"Or, it might put both of us in cells beside him." Mack didn't trust her; he didn't really trust anyone in a badge. "Let's hold off on deciding until we're finished in Manchester. If Uncle Pierce did hide something at his office or home, we might not even need the dodgy detective."

"We'll keep an eye on her anyway." Toshiro grabbed his phone back. "Better to be stabbed in the front than from behind."

"Or, maybe, we don't get stabbed at all?" Mack had no intentions of allowing either of them to get caught in the same situation his father had been. "Stabbing's fucking bad."

"*Language.*" A posh woman from the seat across from them waved her umbrella at him. "Honestly."

Toshiro turned to Mack with mock seriousness. "Hear that, Gregor? Mind your language."

"Right. I'll mind my fucking language, then." Mack couldn't help chuckling at the affronted gasp from across the aisle. "Better behave, or we'll get ourselves in trouble."

"We? I've been a perfect angel."

"The only thing perfect about you is your arse." Mack rolled his eyes when the umbrella made a second appearance with a threatening shake. "Not sure there's anything angelic about you. I do hear the angels sing when I see you starkers."

Toshiro choked for a second before breaking out into a laugh. "An angelic chorus?"

"Every damn night." Mack could've said a lot more about his husband's fine form, but the glare from across the aisle felt like it was boring a hole through his skull. He turned to face the old bat with the umbrella. "Can I help you?"

"*Gregor.*" Toshiro pinched him on the side of the arm. "Leave it alone."

"My apologies. I'll try to restrict myself to the king's English." Mack searched for one of the words Toshiro had told him about from his linguistic studies. "*Tarse.*"

"Gregor."

"What? She is being a dick." He put one of the earbuds attached to his phone and handed the other to Toshiro. *Time for music.* "Wake me up when we get there."

CHAPTER TWENTY-TWO

TOSHIRO

Once in Manchester, they quickly checked into a nondescript hotel close to both Pierce's apartment and office. After a light lunch, they caught a bus to the flat. They made it inside with a crafty bit of lock picking.

"This is odd." Mack drew Toshiro's attention to the switched-off security system. "Pierce's inherited the family paranoia about privacy. Why the bloody hell would he head to London with this disconnected? He knew he'd be arrested."

"No idea." Toshiro had never thought Pierce Siddall to be anything other than overly cautious. "None of this makes any sense at all. Are we really going to find anything with the police having gone over it with a fine-tooth comb?"

"Did I mention family paranoia? He'll have hid something." Mack sounded confident.

Every layer revealed only showed them a hundred more. Toshiro wondered if they'd gotten in over their heads. He wanted to help Pierce, but not at the expense of their own freedom.

"Would it be in bad taste if we made use of his lovely clean sheets on his bed?" Mack stuck his head out of the bedroom ten minutes into their search of the flat. "Is your glare one of interest or revulsion?"

Toshiro pinched the bridge of his nose and drew on his inner well of patience. "Could you focus, Gregor? His neighbours might notice our presence at some point."

"Fine." Mack gave a put-upon sigh when Toshiro muttered insults in Japanese. "Oi. There's no need to be insulting. It was just a suggestion."

"*Focus.*" Toshiro crouched down to continue his inspection of the drawers at the bottom of one of Pierce's many bookshelves. "Why does your uncle have so many damn bookcases? He's got more books than a library. They're all about crime. You'd think he'd want to read something else in his free time."

"He is a detective."

"You'd think he'd try to expand his horizons. We don't read heist novels." Toshiro closed the drawer and moved on to the next. "Well, this is more like it."

"Homemade porn?"

"If you could possibly drag your mind out of the gutter for one second, it would be brilliant." Toshiro eased out a small lockbox from inside the drawer. "Bring your kit over, love, will you?"

To their immense shock, they found family documents and photos inside the box. Toshiro placed a comforting hand on Mack's shoulder while they rifled through the stack of images featuring his husband and his mum. Some dated back to before he'd been born.

"He obviously wanted to remain close even when you didn't want to speak with him." Toshiro lifted up one of the photos; it was one from their small wedding. "Wonder who sent him this one?"

"No idea." Mack slammed the lid shut on the images. "Why didn't he reach out to me?"

"After the last time?" Toshiro carefully returned the box to its cubbyhole. "You didn't exactly make him welcome. I believe your exact words were, 'drop dead, you wanker,' if I recall correctly."

"Not my best moment." Mack dragged his husband into his arms, pressing his face against Toshiro's neck. "Sometimes I can be a bit of a dickhead."

"Yes, you can." Toshiro shifted around to hold Mack tighter. "*Cada dia que passa eu me apaixono mais por você.*"

"Don't know what that means, but it sounds naughty. Was it?" Mack hid a sniffle with a chuckle, but Toshiro heard it anyway.

"Doesn't directly translate, but roughly it means, with every day that passes, I fall in love with you more." He found himself pushed onto his back while Mack swooped in for a hard kiss. "We're not screwing around in your uncle's flat."

"Spoilsport." Mack rolled off him. "I'm almost done in the bedroom. Did you find anything other than his family photos?"

Your family photos, love.

When Mack's father had gotten locked up, Toshiro had noticed him start to distance himself from anything that might remind him of even the concept of family. Photos had immediately gone into storage, as had old letters and journals.

It worried him, but Toshiro didn't quite know how to help Mack. He'd hoped time would heal some of the hurt as it usually did. Pierce's sudden reappearance in their lives had jolted his husband out of it, hopefully for good.

We all need family.

Having a twin meant Toshiro always had someone close to him, a deep family connection even when his mum drove him mad. He and Charlie had been inseparable. He'd found it hard, as a result, to understand Mack willingly forcing Pierce out of his life.

"Tosh?" Mack drew him out of his thoughts. "You'll want to see this."

He followed Mack's voice through the bedroom into the en-suite. "What'd you find?"

Mack held up a sticky note with their names on it. "Cheeky bastard expected us."

The note read in part: *Hello, chaps, here's the password to my computer at the office. Don't fuck in my bed (or anywhere else in my flat). Don't get yourself in trouble.*

Mack held out the packet he'd found with the note in a compartment hidden in the base of the tub. "Think we could get one of these in our bath? It's brilliant."

Amongst other documents, it contained the security

codes and shift changes at the building. Pierce's ID badge was inside the packet as well. It even included a layout of his floor.

Toshiro found it hard to believe Pierce had voluntarily offered them everything required to sneak into his beloved National Crime Agency office. "Is it just me, or does him leaving this for us make you even more paranoid than before?"

"Definitely not just you." Mack inspected the layout. "Wish we'd brought Dom and Charlie with us. Even if we go at night, it'll be tricky."

They cleaned up after themselves and left before any neighbours noticed them to return to the hotel. Getting into the NCA office required serious thought. Neither of them wanted to screw up due to a lack of planning.

Noshing on chips and chicken from Nando's, they dissected the layout Pierce had drawn for them. Toshiro scoured the Internet to find any information on the building. He managed to get a few images from outside that immediately revealed one massive hurdle to their plan.

"CCTV cameras." He pointed them out to Mack, who cursed around the chip in his mouth. "No way Jude can knock them out for long enough for us to get in and out. Never mind they'd notice if their system stopped working even if he could manage it."

"Wouldn't it be brilliant if thieving was like the movies? We could cut the power and sneak in like super-powered ninjas." Mack grabbed yet another chip and held out the plate to offer the last one to Toshiro. "Any great suggestions?

I'm drawing a complete blank."

"I'll message Dom and Charlie. This is way more complicated than we thought. We'll want proper disguises if we're caught on camera." Toshiro rooted around underneath the pile of napkins and papers to find his phone. He briefly chatted via text with his twin. "They're booking tickets now."

"Jude's trying to find a tech solution for us without him actually needing to be here—since we're all completely useless." Mack waved his mobile at Toshiro. "We should've brought them all down with us in the first place. Save us the trouble of waiting."

"While we wait for them, why don't we do some in-person surveillance?" Toshiro refused to trust online photos and a single hand-drawn map. He wanted to see it in person. "We can have a pint afterwards. Did you take your vitamins?"

"Fucking things."

Toshiro hopped off the bed to retrieve the toiletry bag from the en-suite. He tossed three bottles over to Mack. "Take your pills like a good boy."

"*Wanker.*"

He turned his attention to their other mystery—Seeta Joseph. The detective had had quite a career for a such young person. All her commendations made him suspicious of her approaching them for help.

How does she fit in all of this? Is she the crooked copper? If she isn't, why's she talking to a group of villains?

"Tosh?"

He jumped when Mack whacked him in the face with a piece of paper. "What's this say?"

Scanning the printout written in French, Toshiro quickly realised Pierce had been running a secondary investigation outside of the antiquities. *Merde.* He didn't know how to break it to his husband that his uncle believed Rafe Bishop was the reason behind his dad being in prison.

Merde.

Do I go with the truth or the lie?

With Mack?

Always the truth.

CHAPTER TWENTY-THREE

MACK

Deciding to take a shower on his own, Mack stood under the hot water attempting to process his thoughts. Even with their arguments, he'd always believed Rafe could be counted on. He'd never imagined his mentor might sink so low as to murder someone and allow his partner to take the fall for it.

The sound of a belt hitting the floor told him Toshiro had joined him. He watched through the glass door while his husband stripped down. *How does he always know when I need him?*

Toshiro eased up behind him, and his arms went around him. "Let it out, love."

"Not about to go all weepy."

"So you swanned off to shower by yourself for no reason at all?" Toshiro obviously didn't believe a word of it. "I'm sorry about Rafe and your dad."

Mack quirked an eyebrow up in disbelief. "Are you? You've never warmed to Rafe—or trusted him."

"No, I haven't." Toshiro lifted the bar of soap from the dish, getting his fingers covered in suds. He gently began to wash Mack's back. "You cared about him. I might've disliked him, but it doesn't mean I can't appreciate your pain."

"How the fuck could he do that to my dad? They'd worked together for years. He's practically my godfather." Mack knew if his father had been religious at all that Rafe would've been asked immediately. "What else has the bastard done? How idiotically ignorant have I been?"

"Rhetorical question, right?" Toshiro teased. He dipped his fingers down to the cleft of Mack's arse. "We'll get Pierce out—and then your dad as well."

"How?"

"Not a clue."

Pushing his worries out of his mind, Mack focused instead on the slick body behind him. He twisted around to face Toshiro. As he'd avoided desecrating Pierce's flat, he wanted a reward, and the golden magnificence in front of him would work a treat.

He shifted his foot slightly, which turned out to be a mistake. His legs went out from under him, sending both him and Toshiro crashing through the shower door. They landed on the broken glass with water spraying on them. *"Bollocks."*

With a bit of careful manoeuvring, Mack got both of them up out of the glass. He winced when each movement caused the cuts on his back, arse, and legs to twinge. *Fuck.* Toshiro appeared to be mildly better off since he'd landed on top of Mack.

The trip to the nearest A & E was only slightly humiliating. It turned into utter mortification when a bemused Dom and Charlie waited for them in the hotel lobby. They refused to believe their explanation for limping their way towards them.

"Wild sex?" Dom asked once they'd gotten into the lift to go up to their room, a different one from their original.

"Not quite." Mack flipped her off when she snickered at him. "We fell out of the shower."

"You *fell* out of the bath?" Charlie repeated the phrase about six times. "Honestly?"

"You can ask the concierge if you don't believe us." Toshiro leaned gingerly against the wall of the lift. "Broken glass hurts like the dickens in the wrong spots."

Charlie placed a hand on her brother's shoulder. "But it wasn't serious, was it?"

Toshiro patted her hand comfortingly. "Of course not. We'll be right as rain in no time at all."

"Just no buggery?" Dom couldn't help the little prod at them.

Mack dragged his hand roughly through his hair, ignoring how the movement pulled at the bandages on his shoulders. "If you're going to do nothing but tease, you two sod off to your own room and leave us alone."

"To lick your wounds?" Charlie offered one of her rare snarky retorts.

"Not sure they'll be licking a damn thing for a while. Glass cuts take the longest time to heal." Dom slipped her arm around her girlfriend's waist after they'd exited the lift. "Have you eaten? We're starved."

"I could eat." Mack shrugged. He yanked on Toshiro's sleeve to stop the comment he knew would be coming. "Don't say it. I can always eat."

"There's a YO! Sushi around the corner. Why don't Charlie and I pop around to pick up a variety of stuff for us all to nibble on?" Dom suggested.

Mack stopped outside their new room. "Have you dropped your luggage off already?"

"Yep. We're only a few doors down from you." Dom nodded towards their room. "Go on. Find a way to sit comfortably on your sliced bottoms while we get something to fortify your strength."

"Bye." Charlie waved before Dom dragged her back to the lift.

"Oi. Get me two duck bao while you're there," Mack called before the doors slid shut. He hoped Dom had heard him. The meat and pickled cucumber buns were one of his few food addictions since Toshiro introduced them to him. "Right. Into the room. Let's try not to bust any glass in this one."

"Don't worry about the bao. Charlie has a habit of memorising everyone's favourite foods. She'll get you at least three of them." Toshiro limped into the room. He cautiously lowered himself onto one of the two cushioned armchairs in the small seating area across from the bed. "If the pain meds don't kick in soon, I might scratch myself silly. These cuts itch like the devil."

They'd been lectured by the doctor at the hospital. The nurse had laughed at them, particularly as their story of tripping over each other hadn't exactly been believable given the location of some of their injuries. None of the cuts were overly deep, but Mack worried it might affect their plans for the next few days in Manchester.

His luck hadn't held out when it came to falling through the glass. Mack had gotten the worst of the injuries. Toshiro'd be in much better shape for sneaking into Pierce's office.

"We're going to stand out like sore thumbs." Toshiro shifted in the chair and moaned in pain. "They'll notice us limping around."

He had a point.

"Time for a bit of thieving ingenuity." Mack decided against the chair. He stretched out on his side on the bed after finding an angle without any cuts. "Or, we convince Dom and Charlie to do it for us."

"Not the worst idea you've ever had." Toshiro twisted his arm to look at one of the many bandages. "Want to know what *is* the worst?"

"No."

CHAPTER TWENTY-FOUR

The infiltration into the Interpol branch in Manchester went far more smoothly than imagined. Dom and Charlie managed to sneak into Pierce's office with little trouble. They'd been helped along by what Dom referred to as "an annoying but dashing black detective who kept flirting with Charlie."

Trev Elywn.

A short internet search showed him to be a detective only recently assigned to the British Interpol office. He'd worked with Pierce for a while, and the man had recommended him for the promotion. Toshiro wondered if perhaps Trev Elwyn wanted to repay Pierce by helping; he clearly had to have known who they were to provide a distraction for Charlie and Dom.

It still made Toshiro uneasy. They now had two detectives colluding with them. He found the help more than a little suspicious.

"Toshi?" Charlie twisted around on her piano bench and snapped her fingers to draw his attention. "Were you even listening?"

"Sorry." He'd come over to spend time with her while Mack drove up to see his dad. "Play it again for me?"

Charlie wandered over to sit on the floor next to him. "What's wrong?"

"Too many coppers inserting themselves into our lives." Toshiro rested his head against her shoulder. "What did you think about Trev?"

"Odd."

"How so?" Toshiro had learned over the years that his sister might miss things because of her autism, but being autistic also led her to unusual insights into people's characters. "What made him odd other than the whole not arresting you part?"

Charlie grabbed her fidget cube from her pocket. "Actually, that was super odd."

"Great hero name. Super Odd."

"You're an idiot." Charlie laughed behind her hand. "Forgot what I was going to say. Damn it."

"Sorry." Toshiro felt an immediate sense of guilt. His sister struggled at times to hold on to a thought, and interrupting her mid-conversation often had the consequence of causing her to lose track of what she wanted to say. "I'm a horrible brother."

"No." Charlie shook her head. "Just an idiot."

"Thanks."

While Charlie returned to her piano playing, Toshiro

stretched his legs out and returned to considering the confusing labyrinth of the mysterious coppers. The infiltration of Pierce's office had gone smoothly but had been pointless. His computer was gone, along with the majority of his files.

They'd had nothing to show for all of it. The entire trip to Manchester had been mostly nothing more than a pain in the arse. *Literally and figuratively.* Dom and Charlie continued to laugh at the massive number of bandages covering both him and his husband.

No more shower sex.

Ever.

Well, maybe not never, let's not get overly dramatic.

"He's too smiley."

Toshiro glanced over to find his sister had stopped playing and spun around on her bench to face him. "Who?"

"Elwyn."

"Ahh. Genuine or fake smiley?"

"Not sure." Charlie shrugged. "Could be fake. Ask Dom. She's better at seeing it. I've never met a detective who smiled so much before. They're usually broody like Mack when you make him sleep on the couch."

"Charlie."

"What? He goes all sad puppy dog eyes." Charlie twisted back around to face her piano. "Go away now, please."

With a wry chuckle, Toshiro got to his feet, kissed his sister on the top of the head, and headed out of the music room. He found Dom in her art room; the rain made working in the garden impossible. She was working on a watercolour on a large canvas.

"Did she kick you out then?" Dom dropped her brush in a jar with a few others and set her palette to one side. "Surprised she lasted so long, to be honest. She's been a bit quiet since we got back from Manchester. Think she needs a few quiet days to recover."

"Think we all need a few days to recover." Toshiro was glad his cuts continued to heal well, but they itched terribly. "She claimed Elywn was too smiley."

Dom wiped her hands on her apron, motioning for him to follow her out of the room. "Forced is the word I would use. He tried too hard to help—to flirt as well. It didn't seem genuine to me, though. He wasn't honestly trying to get either of our numbers."

Layers of oddness stacked upon a mystery combined with a serious cluster of we're about to get royally screwed but have no idea by whom.

"Another person to investigate?"

Toshiro dragged his hand roughly through his hair. "Can't we get back to being robbers? It was way more fun. I'm heading out. I'll let you know what Mack found out from his dad."

"Tosh?"

He stopped in the hall on the way to the front door. "Dom."

She rolled her eyes at him. "Have you considered the people who screwed Mack's dad over might be the same ones going after Pierce?"

"After so many years?"

"The same name keeps popping up in all of this."

Toshiro knew precisely who she was talking about. "Rafe Bishop."

"Exactly." She shoved her hands into her pockets and continued walking him down the hall towards the door. "Is Mack honestly prepared to face it if Rafe does turn out to be the one who framed his dad?"

"Yes," Toshiro lied through his teeth. He didn't believe Mack had really faced the truth of the situation. "He'll be fine."

"And *you* are the shittiest liar. So you might want to work on it." Dom nodded towards the door. "Bye."

Flipping her off, Toshiro darted out the door before she decided to throw paint at him. His plan to relax and catch up on his writing deadlines failed miserably. He found Seeta Joseph sitting on a bench a few steps away from their loft.

What now?

He tried to just ignore her, but she followed him to the door. "Can I do something for you, Detective? Can you make it quick? I'm busy."

"Pierce Siddall went missing from custody." Seeta dropped the bomb on him. "Quick enough for you?"

Shit.

"I've never voluntarily invited the police into my home." Toshiro hesitated by the electronic lock to his home. "And I'm not sure I want to start now."

"What do you have to lose?"

CHAPTER TWENTY-FIVE

MACK

Sitting in his borrowed vehicle of the week, Mack tried to process the brief conversation with his father. He hadn't reacted well to the questions about Rafe. It brought their visit to an abrupt end.

When Mack had mentioned what they found on Rafe, his father had told him to leave it alone. He'd also called for the officer to take him to his cell. *What the hell is going on?*

He wanted to be home with his Toshiro who always made sense out of everything. "What the actual fuck is going on?"

The return drive to London felt longer than the first one when his dad had just been locked up. Mack wanted it to be over—to be gone. His desperation to be home naturally led to his getting stuck in a traffic jam for two hours.

Stepping into the loft, Mack found his day had one last surprise for him. He found Toshiro sitting across from Seeta Joseph at the breakfast table having tea. His husband took one look at his face, excused himself from the table, and walked over to drag him over to the privacy of their bedroom.

"We just left a police officer in our house unsupervised." Mack thought he'd dealt with enough surprises for one day.

"What's happened?" Toshiro eased Mack into a hug, holding him tightly. "You looked totally shattered when you came in."

"I'm fine."

"No, you're not." He refused to release Mack from his embrace. "Is your dad worse?"

"Not quite." Mack had thought his father seemed healthier than the last visit. "He refused to talk to me about Rafe. Told me to leave it the fuck alone."

"Really?" Toshiro sounded as stunned as Mack had been. "Why has everything suddenly gone weird on us?"

"No idea, but I'd like it to stop now." Mack sunk into his husband's arms, looping his own around Toshiro. He dropped his forehead onto his husband's shoulder. "I don't understand. If he didn't do it, why wouldn't my dad talk to me about it? He's told me everything else about his life, even shit I'd rather he kept to himself."

"Maybe he's scared of what might happen to you?" Toshiro suggested after they'd stood embracing each other in silence for a minute. "If your dad has dirt on Rafe, he knows how dangerous he can be, right? You're his only son; he likely doesn't want to risk you getting hurt."

"By not talking to me?"

"You're a stubborn git. He knows it because I imagine he's one as well," Toshiro teased. "Now, I love you, but we've bigger issues than paternal ones at the mo'."

"Oh?"

"The police detective sergeant seated in our kitchen?"

"Right. Why the fuck did you let her into the house for?" Mack couldn't believe Toshiro had voluntarily allowed her inside. "Did she threaten you?"

"Not quite."

He released Toshiro from his arms. "Well, let's not keep her waiting. She might decide to get nosy, and I'd rather not worry about getting arrested in the middle of a mystery."

"You're not going to decide to be Sherlock Holmes, are you? Robin Hood is bad enough." Toshiro tugged on Mack's beard with a grin. "You used to smoke a pipe."

"Until Charlie started sneezing every time I even thought about bringing it out." Mack didn't mind so much. He enjoyed one good smoke of tobacco every year but left it alone to avoid setting his sister-in-law's allergies off. "Poor woman."

Returning to the kitchen, they found Seeta in the same exact spot, still drinking her tea. Mack suspiciously glanced around the room to see if anything had been moved. If he'd been in her position, he'd have taken the opportunity to peek in the drawers at the least.

"What's going on then?" Mack leaned against the counter, preferring not to sit after having been on his arse all day. He had one cut in particular that still hurt a bit and driving hadn't helped at all. "You're risking a lot by colluding with us."

"You've never been arrested," Seeta pointed out.

"I've no doubts CID has a thick file on us even though they've never managed to prove a thing." Mack knew for a fact they had one; he'd seen it. "Why are you here?"

"I went to pay Pierce a visit, as they'd told me his transfer was delayed. They've let me in to see him without issue previously so I figured why not try again. This time, they turned me away. I managed to find out they lied about moving him." Seeta paused, a bit dramatically in Mack's opinion, before continuing. "Trouble is no one seems to know where he went. Procedures have to be followed when an investigation involves a detective. They can't just drag him off never to be seen from again."

"They do in the movies."

Mack grinned at his husband, though Seeta didn't appear to find as much appreciation in the humour. "Maybe they took him for an interrogation? Isn't that what you detective types do?"

"I thought so as well until I heard my chief inspector and superintendent talking with several of the Interpol officers about keeping his disappearance under wraps. They didn't know where he'd gone either. The CCTV cameras were turned off. It's like he vanished into thin air—but no one is investigating to find out where he went." She clutched at her cup of tea nervously. "Look, he's a good man."

Mack stared intently at her trying to read her body language. She didn't have the experience yet to mask the way his uncle did. "How long have you been in love with him?"

"I'm not." Seeta almost dropped the cup halfway to her lips. "I'd never. He's—"

"So, that's a yes. Listen, love, you're obviously in the

wrong profession. You're a terrible liar, and you've the worst poker face I've ever seen. Do they let you interrogate criminals?" Mack instantly felt guilty for the tease when she seemed to be fighting back a sniffle. "*Shit*. Sorry. Don't cry."

"I'm not weeping, you arse, I've had a cold for days." She scowled at him and set the cup down with a heavy thud. "My feelings for Pierce are none of your business. I've never shared them with him, so I'm certainly not about to do so with his cheeky nephew. Do you want to help me or not?"

"Not."

"Yes, of course." Toshiro pierced his husband with a glare, and Mack felt himself wilt a bit under the glare. "We're capable of putting our differences aside to help your uncle."

"Well, obviously," Mack said with a confidence he didn't feel.

Over several pots of tea and two packets of biscuits, the unlikely trio hammered out how best to approach determining first where Pierce had been taken and then getting him out. Seeta promised to keep them informed. Mack kicked his husband in the shin to prevent him from making one on their behalf.

He couldn't help the immense feeling of relief when she left. "Right. I'm going to need a drink to process this bizarre day."

"Why don't we have pints and sit outside? It's lovely and not raining for once." Toshiro pushed him towards the doors that led out to their small terrace.

Mack collapsed back onto one of the loungers to stare up at the sky. "*Fuck.*"

"Assume Rafe's involved." Toshiro handed him one of the cans of beer and took the seat beside him. "Assume he, by some sort of villain miracle, got to Pierce in custody."

"*Toshi.*"

"Just hypothetically, all right?"

Mack didn't think at this point there was anything hypothetical about it, but he didn't want to say it out loud—not yet. "Go on, then."

"Where would Rafe keep him? Skip the whole plausibility of it all. If he's got your uncle, where's he put him?" Toshiro stared up at the slowly darkening sky. "Not at his house. He's arrogant, but not stupid."

Assuming Pierce hasn't been murdered.

"The grotto," Mack murmured absently to himself.

"The what?"

"An old gothic ruin the Bishop family has owned for centuries. I called it the grotto because I didn't know what one was. I thought it was a dark, wet place. I played in it as a child when my dad and Rafe were best mates." Mack hadn't thought about the medieval monstrosity in years. "Used to scare the shit out of me. It even had a dungeon hidden underneath the collapsed main part of the castle."

"A dungeon?"

"I got trapped in it once. Rafe had to rescue me." Mack remembered being terrified of dying in the cramped cell with water dripping on him. "It'd be the perfect place to cause someone to disappear."

"Why don't we get up in the morning to drive out? We'll get Dom and Charlie to go with us." Toshiro stretched his arm out to take Mack's hand. "You going to be okay?"

Mack knew his husband meant would he be okay if it ended up with Rafe being involved in all of it. "I'll have to be, won't I?"

Toshiro squeezed his hand tightly. "We'll figure it out together."

CHAPTER TWENTY-SIX

TOSHIRO

It was a cold, grey, dreary morning. The sun hadn't come up yet. Their quartet shivered in the damp grass and mud half a mile from the castle ruins in the middle of the forest, glaring into the hot drinks they'd picked up at a café on the way through Aylesbury.

"Are we sure he's not here?" Dom had an arm around Charlie, who hated both morning and cold days.

"We'll find out momentarily." Toshiro held up the drone Jude had lent to them. "I'll do a check for CCTV cameras as well. If I don't crash it."

He didn't crash it, thankfully. Jude would've killed him for ruining his new toy. They managed to spot one camera along with fresh tire tracks in the mud leading towards the area where Mack remembered the dungeon entrance being.

Right.

Camera first.

Deciding on a low-tech solution, they merely snuck in

on the camera's blind side and covered it. The odds of Rafe or anyone else monitoring the footage constantly were slim to none. He'd arrogantly assume his plans would continue on without issue.

Even so, the four all agreed to move as quickly as possible. One reason they'd left their vehicle so far from the property was to avoid any chance of Rafe realising who'd been there. *For now.* Toshiro didn't believe it would take long for him to at least suspect Mack.

"Mack?"

Toshiro spun around at the worried tone in his twin's voice. He jogged quickly towards one of the more extensive section of the ruined castle to find Mack feverishly moving the stone, brick, and other debris aside. "Gregor?"

"It's down here somewhere."

With an exasperated sigh at his husband's stubbornness, Toshiro waved the others over to help. Mack had gotten cut worse than he had in Manchester. The last thing either of them needed was to make their healing injuries worse.

"Here." Mack dropped the last stone behind them, ignoring how it rolled down to hit him on the shoe. His fingers traced a rusted iron handle attached to a wooden panel. "If it's as heavy as I remember, I'm going to need a hand."

It turned out not to be as heavy as Mack recalled, his strength having obviously improved with age. They yanked hard, the door lifted up, and they fell on their arses. Toshiro flipped his sister and her girlfriend off before his husband dragged him up to his feet.

"Who's going first?" Dom asked.

Charlie crept up to stare down into the hole in the ground, holding the torches they'd brought with them. "Not it."

Dom stepped back with her hands up. "Not it, either."

Toshiro glanced over at his husband who took a step away as well. "You're all children. Cowardly little youths."

Snatching one of the flashlights from his twin, Toshiro hesitated before stepping onto the first rung of the ladder leading down into the darkness. He kept one hand firmly on the railing while the other held the torch tightly. The other three shone theirs down as well to give a clearer view.

He had to bend down to keep from whacking his head on the roughly hewn ceiling of the dungeon. It took several minutes for Mack to join him. Dom and Charlie stayed up top to ensure no one locked them inside.

Taking the lead, Toshiro stretched his arm out to grab Mack's hand. He hoped it would keep his husband from tripping over everything. The tunnel got smaller before it reached what had once been the cells of a medieval dungeon.

"Well, bit creepy." Toshiro shone the light into the first three and found nothing but dust, spiders, and rats. He found what appeared to be bones in the fourth. "More than a bit. Was that there the last time?"

"I tried not to look." Mack visibly shuddered. "Check the last one."

"Nothing." Toshiro felt equally relieved and disappointed. He'd worried they'd find Pierce's body, but finding nothing made him even more concerned. "What now?"

"One more spot to look at." Mack pointed his flashlight

towards a partially caved-in wall. "If you squeeze through there, you'll find one last cell. It's where I got stuck as a kid."

"Me?" Toshiro peered into the dimly lit area at his husband. "You okay?"

Mack twisted around before crouching down to sift around in the dirt. "I can't see."

Shit.

Toshiro ran his fingers through his husband's wavy hair, brushing out a few cobwebs. "Let me see if I find anything. I'll be right back."

After shifting stone that appeared recently moved, Toshiro climbed through into the cavity behind. He coughed through the dirt kicked up by his slithering around. Turning the torch up to the highest brilliance, he scanned the area, and his heart stopped.

Merde.

Paska.

Cachu.

Mierda.

Shit.

And any other damn version of shit I know.

"Gregor? Can you hear me? I need you to get back to the ladder. Tell Dom to bring me the first aid kit. She's got the most experience with triaging injuries. Get Charlie to reach Jude. He's got that doctor friend who makes house calls off the record." Toshiro shouted through the hole. "Call Seeta Joseph. She has to know a few trustworthy people."

"Toshi?"

"He's alive, Mack. Barely." Toshiro didn't know enough to actually assess Pierce's condition. "*Hurry.*"

CHAPTER TWENTY-SEVEN

MACK

By the time Mack made it the short distance to the ladder, he'd smacked his head on the ceiling and wall three times. His feet tripped over rocks he simply couldn't see on the ground. Anger surged through him at his inability to see clearly.

The beam from the flashlight acted like a tunnel within the tunnel to his vision. A stark reminder of what would likely happen as his vision grew progressively worse. Mack shook his head and pushed through his fear-driven frustration.

"Dom?"

"Macky Mack?" she yelled down at him. "You okay?"

"Get your first aid kit." Mack took a breath to steel himself before stowing the torch in his pocket to begin the climb to the top. His fingers clung painfully to the rungs of the ladder, unable to make out shapes in the dark. He hated how his mind tumbled towards panic. The two women waited for him looking anxiously when he climbed out. "Think you can brave the descent? Toshi's going to need help, and I can't do it."

Charlie hugged her girlfriend and pressed the first aid kit into her arms. "Good luck."

"*Thanks*." Dom glared at both of them.

The wait was agonising. Mack distracted himself by contacting first Jude, and then Seeta. He didn't want to reach out to the detective, but if anyone would help Pierce, hopefully she would.

Within an hour, a team of officers and medics had arrived, and Seeta had overruled his plan to keep it off-record, claiming it would do more harm than good to proving Pierce's innocence. *Well, if Rafe is watching the area, he's going to notice all this activity.* They managed to get Pierce up to ground level by strapping him to a board and using a series of ropes to stabilise it. Mack's heart dropped at the state of his uncle.

He'd been beaten. *And fuck knows what else.* Mack made a promise to himself to ruin Rafe for it. He had zero doubts his former mentor was directly involved.

Not willing to fully trust anyone other than his crew, Mack sent Toshiro in the ambulance with his uncle. He went with Seeta. Dom promised to follow with Charlie after they finished replacing the stones over the entrance and covering up the footprints and vehicle tracks.

It might help.

Doubtful.

The truth was Mack had no doubt Rafe would know

he'd been involved. Who else could trace the connection between his mentor and his uncle? *Just me. The fucking bastard. I'll ruin him for doing this to Pierce, and for what he did to my dad.*

They followed the ambulance to a nearby village surgeon. In a truly weird coincidence, Seeta had apparently grown up in the area and developed a close relationship with both the local police and doctor, who turned out to be her mother. After a nurse kicked him out of the room for hovering, Mack paced outside by the vehicle, waiting anxiously for Dom and Charlie and ignoring Toshiro's attempts to reassure him.

"Sir?"

Mack came to such a sudden stop he almost tipped over. He found a young woman by the door. "Yes?"

"The doctor has him stable. She wanted to give you an update." She held the door open to allow them through.

Mack took the hand Toshiro held out to him and raced into the building with him. They found the doctor having a hushed conversation with Seeta. "How is he?"

"Badly injured, but stable. I suggested a hospital but my Seeta says he'll be safer here, and I'd rather not move him in any case." Dr Joseph talked them through the damage done to his uncle in the short amount of time Rafe had him. She explained her treatment plans then returned to her patient, leaving them alone in the hallway with her daughter.

"Good news or bad news first?"

"Good." Mack didn't fully trust Seeta, but his suspicions had all but disappeared. "I could use something positive."

"They've decided Pierce is innocent. I can't say for certain who did it, not with enough evidence to convince anyone, but your uncle is safe from prosecution. More than that, he'll have a security detail until we've caught them." Seeta waved them down the hall away to an empty exam room. "Bad news? We've no idea who did this."

"No idea?" Mack queried in disbelief.

"None." Seeta tugged on her earlobe while nodding towards the closed door. "The investigation is officially being closed into your uncle's disappearance. It would be best if you allowed Interpol and CID to handle any further issues."

"*Right.*" Mack wondered if they'd all fallen into some bizarre alternate universe. "We'll go sit with my uncle, then."

As they stepped by her to the door, Seeta caught Toshiro by the arm. He bent his head, and Mack couldn't quite hear the brief whispered conversation. His husband nodded to her sharply before taking Mack's hand to lead him out of the room.

"What the hell was that?" Mack kept his voice low, easing past a frowning nurse towards his uncle's room.

"Later." Toshiro motioned towards the gathered group of uniformed and plainclothes police at the front of the surgery. "Why don't you check on Pierce? I'm going to step outside to see what's keeping Dom and Charlie. They should've at least texted by now."

They exchanged a worried glance and a quick kiss before Toshiro ducked out the door. Mack eased the door open and stepped into the room to see his uncle unconscious on the bed. He wanted to make a quick exit but forced himself to continue inside.

"Well, you look like shit." Mack dragged a chair from by the door over to the bed and got comfortable in it. He almost immediately shot to his feet. "Right. Get well."

Rushing from the room, Mack darted by Seeta, who appeared to be briefing her colleagues. He found Toshiro on the phone in a heated argument with Dom. *What now? Can't we have one sodding break?*

Toshiro held a finger up to stop Mack from interrupting. "No, Oi, Dominica, you listen to me. You two are not chasing down some shit Jude claims to have found on Rafe and Mary. You wait for us."

Mack reached out to take the phone only for Toshiro to deflect his hand easily. "Let me talk to her."

"No, Dom. I'm not…. Will you listen to me for once?" Toshiro twisted away from Mack's hand. He went off in Japanese first and then Portuguese. "I don't care if you don't understand me. Put Charlie on the phone. I want to talk to my sister."

"Tosh."

His husband flung his phone at the ground with a muttered curse. "She hung up on me."

"I'm writing this down so we can remember you had a temper tantrum for the next time you tell me to stop being a child. I can point out you broke your phone after an argument." Mack bent down to grab the mobile. He dusted it off, wincing at the cracked screen. "Think it still works.

What happened?"

"Jude tracked the Wi-Fi connection from the CCTV camera at the ruins. He believes it will lead to Rafe and Mary." Toshiro snatched his phone back and tried to turn it on. "Dom and Charlie decided to check out the address without us."

"It's not like they're helpless. They could probably kick both of our arses with one hand tied behind their backs." Mack had a healthy respect for their capabilities having seen them in action. He knew his husband did as well, so he didn't quite understand his overreaction. "You're not generally prone to flying off the handle, Tosh."

"They've gone off alone and unarmed to face someone who isn't alone and happens to be heavily armed." Toshiro messed around with his phone until it finally turned on. "I'd argue with you if you wanted just the two of us to confront Rafe."

"They'll...."

Toshiro grabbed Mack by the front of his shirt, dragging him forward. "I know he was your mentor and all, and despite how pissed you are, you're trying to cling to happy memories. But you've got to face facts. He's dangerous. He's murdered at least one person we know of, tried to kill another, and he's framed two people. What do you think he's capable of doing to anyone else who gets in his way?"

Fair point.

Well, shit.

"Wait. What was all the whispering with Seeta?" Mack decided the conversation about Rafe wasn't getting them anywhere.

"She's been sidelined. Someone, obviously the actual dirty cop, managed to get the investigation shut down. She's going to make *quiet* inquiries into it." Toshiro stepped back from Mack. "What are we going to do about Rafe?"

"Not a damn clue."

CHAPTER TWENTY-EIGHT

They'd made it halfway to London before Mack's phone buzzed. Toshiro grabbed it to check the message for his husband since he sat behind the wheel. They'd *borrowed* a vehicle since Dom and Charlie had their car.

Rafe: I believe it's time for us to converse like adults.

"Can you believe this wanker?" Toshiro read the message out to his husband who rolled his eyes in response. "What do we do?"

"Converse like adults." Mack pulled over onto the shoulder and grabbed his phone. "Maybe it'll buy some time to talk Charlie and Dom into waiting."

Mack: With words? Seemed as though you'd moved on to brute force. Not very civilised of you, Rafe.

Rafe: Don't be childish, Gregor. I'm at my family's estate in Hertfordshire. The one along the river. Meet me at 9pm at the lodge down the lane from the main house.

Bastard.

Does he think he's a Bond villain?

"His family estate?" Mack flipped the phone off. "It's not his family estate. It came from my mum's side. He fucking stole it from my dad before he got arrested."

The theft of property that should've been his had actually been the beginning of the rift between Mack and his mentor. The house and land weren't massive by any stretch of the imagination. It had been the only thing Mack's mum left them when she died.

"Another crime to put at his feet." Toshiro thought Rafe had gotten away with a lot over the years.

It didn't take a genius to figure out why Rafe wanted to meet in the evening. Darkness made everything harder for Mack. Toshiro knew the man revelled in picking apart his opponents' weakness.

"Text Dom. She'll have to drive." Mack tossed his phone at Toshiro, pulling the vehicle back onto the road. "We'll go together."

The silence grew heavy in the vehicle. Toshiro had a rushed text argument with his twin and her girlfriend before they agreed to meet up at Jude's place. They needed to regroup and come up with some semblance of a plan.

"Gregor?"

"Don't," Mack said tightly.

Toshiro hated the way the slow degradation of Mack's sight seemed to erode away his husband's confidence and humour as well. "We'll manage."

"You can't drive. What happens when I'm no longer able

to do so either? Uber?" Mack whacked his hand against the steering wheel in obvious frustration. "I'm useless."

"I didn't marry you for your driving skills." Toshiro rested his hand on Mack's thigh. "And I've been taking classes."

"Classes?"

"Learning how to drive." Toshiro had planned to surprise Mack on their wedding anniversary. "I've a test in a couple of weeks."

"You hate driving."

"I do."

Mack stared at him for long enough that Toshiro reached out to turn his face back towards the road. "You seriously loathe driving to the depths of your soul."

"I wasn't that dramatic," Toshiro retorted.

"You were."

Toshiro pinched Mack's thigh through his trousers. "I love you more than I hate driving. So stop worrying about Uber."

They arrived at Jude's flat not long after Charlie and Dom. His sister glared at him. *Brilliant.* Toshiro scrubbed his fingers across his face tiredly; it was never easy to explain himself to his sister when she'd dug her heels in stubbornly.

Waving Charlie over, Toshiro pulled her into Jude's bedroom to try to smooth things over. His twin took stubbornness to insane levels when slighted. Finding Pierce had scared him, though, and he had no doubts Rafe was capable of taking all of them out if necessary.

"Well?" Charlie perched on the edge of Jude's bed with her arms stiffly at her side. "I'm angry."

"I know."

"I'm angry."

Toshiro sat on the opposite side of the bed from her to give her space but not loom over her either. "I wasn't doubting your abilities."

"You...."

"I know you're hacked off at me, but Rafe is dangerous. I wouldn't go in alone myself. We stick together. It's the best plan—the only way to survive this." Toshiro watched in relief as Charlie wilted a little. "I'm sorry I shouted at Dom."

"And me."

"Mostly at Dom."

"You cursed."

"So did she," Toshiro pointed out.

"You were angry." Charlie hunched in on herself. She never did well with the louder emotions.

"Not angry. Worried." Toshiro scratched at his side as one of his almost healed cuts was irritated by his shirt shifting slightly. "Sometimes when you're concerned about someone you love, it comes out a bit panicked."

"Angry."

Toshiro risked inching further along the edge of the bed until he sat beside his sister. "Not angry, definitely not with you. I promise."

"Felt angry." Charlie often struggled with separating out the subtleties of emotions. She lumped them into categories, which occasionally led to issues with defining them. "You sure?"

"Most definitely. Hug?" Toshiro opened his arms, leaving the decision to her. "No hug?"

"Hug." She fell into his arms. "Is Mack's uncle going to be okay?"

"Think so." Toshiro rested his chin on her head. "Why don't we join the others to plot how we're going to teach Rafe a lesson?"

"And not die?"

He couldn't help the slight sense of apprehension slithering up his spine. "And not dying would be brilliant."

CHAPTER TWENTY-NINE

MACK

Well, I've mucked this up brilliantly, haven't I?

Yes, yes I have.

Mack sat on the damp, cold ground in the middle of God knows where trying to see in the dark. He'd lost his phone so had no way to create light or call for help. "*Fuck.*"

As a teenager, Mack had loved darkness. He'd used it too frequently to make his earliest jobs easier. The further his night blindness had progressed, the less he'd enjoyed it.

The truth of his disability had never struck him fully in the face until now. His husband—his family in danger and Mack could do nothing but stumble around in a field unable to see. In the darkness without lamps or a flashlight, everything blurred as his vision closed in on him.

It felt as though he looked through an out-of-focus camera in a dimly lit room. As twilight faded into night, even the slight hints of shadows had disappeared leaving him in darkness. In his youth, his eyes would eventually adjust; they'd stopped doing that a year ago.

In the city with so many street lamps, the night didn't affect him as much. He used the brightness to provide a guide for him. Being out in the country was a different story.

Is this what I have to look forward to when it's all gone?

It had all gone wrong the minute they stepped inside the building. Mack had been the last to enter. The second he crossed the threshold, he felt a massive pain in the back of his head, then nothing.

He'd woken up face down on the grass with an aching head. His phone had been taken along with the pocket knife and locking kit usually kept in his pockets. He'd tried to get to his feet to head towards the lodge only to realise he'd no idea how to get there.

And if I did know the direction, I can't see to fucking find my way.

What if they've hurt my Toshi?

Right.

Getting to his hands and knees, Mack crawled in the general direction he'd heard a door slam. The sound had been what woke him up. He'd find his way—he had to.

If Mack squinted, his vision improved slightly, though only for short periods. He moved painfully slowly to what appeared to be a structure. *Hopefully the right sodding one.* He dragged himself across the rough ground through at least one cowpat, but stubborn determination kept him going.

He would not give up.

He'd rather face Rafe and whoever had helped him blindly than lie on the cold ground waiting for the inevitable.

The night grew even darker as clouds obscured the moonlight. Mack had the first bit of hope when the damp grass turned into gravel. He knew then he'd found one of the driveways, and picked up the pace, ignoring the pain from the rocks digging into his palms and knees.

He'd tried walking, but every other step ended with him tripping. Vertigo also became a problem. His lack of vision disoriented him completely, keeping him on his knees for safety.

All of the lights from the main property and surrounding buildings had been turned off. Mack had no doubt Rafe intended for it to cripple him in the darkness. He moved off the gravel, keeping a hand on the edge between the lawn and the road to keep him from straying too far from it.

A muffled cry froze him mid-crawl. Mack sat up on his heels, listening for another sound, anything at all to give him a direction to go. Time slowed agonisingly while he waited.

Come on. Give me something, for God's sake. I'm fucking crawling blind here.

Quite literally.

He heard it again, amidst the sounds of the country at night, a slightly muffled sobbing. Not knowing who might be around, he worked to stay as silent as possible. He eventually reached the structure his eyes had managed to pick out from a distance—not the lodge or the main house, but the stables.

Easing the wooden gate open, Mack snuck inside the stable. He thanked all his lucky stars that Rafe had stopped keeping horses on the property. Their neighing would've immediately drawn attention to his presence.

A hitch in the sobbing told him instantly who'd been left in one of the stalls. Mack followed the crying to the far end of the stable. The door had been locked from the outside with a padlock.

Shit.

Think, Mack, c'mon. You've been picking locks like this one since you were a kid.

Sitting down by the door, Mack ran his fingers along the heel of his left boot. He kept a single pick hidden in a gap in the sole. It had gotten him out of more than one tight spot over the years.

With an intense amount of effort, Mack managed to work from just the sound and feel of the lock. His many years of experience came in handy when it eventually sprang apart. He slipped the bar across, allowing the door to swing open.

"*Mack?*" Charlie's watery gasp proved his suspicion correct. "You're not dead."

"Not yet," Mack whispered, inching forward towards her. "Can't see too well at the moment."

"They took Dom and Toshi." Charlie grabbed his arm; her fingers clutched at him even through her trembling. "Mary said they didn't need the blind git and the…."

Mack had no doubts whatever had been said about Charlie had been vile. "I'd give you a hug, but I'm covered in cow shit at the moment."

"They've all gone." Charlie fell into his arms anyway. Her fingers gripped his shirt tight enough Mack had to tilt his chin up to get air. "Heard the footsteps and cars leave. Took my phone and my fidget cube. The wankers. Why'd they take Toshi and Dom?"

"Not a fucking clue." Mack sat on the ground with his back against the wall. "You're going to have to guide me towards one of the houses. If they've got power, the phones should be on as well. We've got to try to reach Jude—and probably Seeta as well for help."

"Not Trev," Charlie said firmly. "He's the one who bashed you on the head. Knew he was too smiley."

What a fucking mess this all is.

What did I drag my family into this time?

If he's hurt Tosh or Dom... I'll end Rafe and whoever else is with them.

Charlie whacked him on the arm. "Positive thoughts. Think positive thoughts. They'll be fine. They have to be fine. You hear me?"

Mack held her tightly and decided not to break her heart with the truth. Rafe had a ruthlessness when it came to his money. "We'll find them."

I only hope they're alive and well when we do.

Fuck.

CHAPTER THIRTY

TOSHIRO

Well, this has gone absolutely tits up on us, hasn't it?

Stuffed in the boot of a BMW, Toshiro had Dom's high-heeled boots shoved in his face and a tire iron digging into his side. They'd been gagged and tied up. It gave him far too much time to think about the sickening thud as Trev Elywn, detective inspector, had smashed his husband over the head with the butt of his pistol.

They'd been outnumbered and outgunned. *Might have to rethink not carrying a weapon of some sort.* Toshiro had never been quite as helpless as when he'd been forced to do nothing while his husband and his sister were dragged off. The sound of two gunshots not long after left him enraged and heartbroken.

The scream from Dom would probably echo in his mind for years to come. Toshiro had been impotent in his anger with a gun to his forehead. Lying in the car boot, he chose to believe Mack and Charlie hadn't been killed.

Gunshots don't mean anything.

Okay, time to be proactive, if—no, they aren't dead, so you've got to ensure you and Dom make it out of this as well.

With a bit of effort, Toshiro shifted around a bit to get the rope on his wrist on the sharp edge of the tire iron. He dragged over and over, ignoring the way it dug into his skin. Bloody or not, he wanted his hands free.

If nothing else, I'll feel less helpless.

Toshiro eventually managed to work his hands free. He yanked the fabric from his mouth and wiggled around until he could help free Dom. "You okay?"

"No, I'm not fucking okay," Dom hissed at him. "For all we know, Charlie and Mack are dead in the dirt."

"We don't know that for sure." Toshiro refused to abandon hope. "Think we can get the boot open?"

"And what? Jump out on the motorway?"

"Someone will notice two people trapped in a boot on the motorway, Dom, even if it's in the dark." Toshiro ran his fingers along until he found the latch, then followed the release cables to the emergency release. "What kind of idiotic wanker shoves someone into the boot of a car but doesn't bother to break the tab that'll open it?"

"Does it matter?" Dom nudged him with her foot. "Get on with it."

"It's about to get really windy." Toshiro watched her grab a hold of the tire iron. "Fingers crossed."

Seconds before Toshiro went to tug on the release, the vehicle slowed and veered off the motorway. They held their breaths when it eventually came to a stop. He could hear voices and other cars starting and stopping.

"What's that sound?" Dom tilted her head up as though trying to get closer to the seam. "Fuck. I think we're at a petrol station."

"The second it's open. We get out, and we run inside. They won't risk drawing attention to themselves. We've got to get a hold of Seeta." Toshiro thanked all his lucky stars, nodded to Dom, and yanked hard on the release. "Leave the tire iron. Might give the wrong impression."

Scrambling out of the boot, Toshiro helped Dom out, stumbling as their stiff limbs refused to cooperate. They instantly came face-to-face with one of Rafe's hired muscle. He'd started towards them, drawing his weapon out from under his shirt, when a shout of "Oi, what do think you're doing then?" drew their attention.

Toshiro grabbed Dom by the arm, dragging her as they both limped painfully around the petrol pump towards the two rather large, muscled men who'd called out. "Anyone have a mobile? Can you call the police? Please? We need help. We were kidnapped."

Dom immediately joined in the conversation, trying to push people into action. "They've still got his sister and husband captive."

Rafe's thugs, who'd been next to the BMW, leapt into it and sped off so quickly the vehicle fishtailed slightly on a turn. Toshiro breathed only a slight sigh of relief. They might be safe, but what about Mack and Charlie?

The next hour flew by for them. With a borrowed mobile,

Toshiro called Seeta. Dom managed to talk the witnesses into not calling the local police. One of the petrol station attendants brought them hot tea and sandwiches.

After a brief but heated conversation, Seeta promised to send a car around to pick them up. She was closer to the estate so she would head directly there. Toshiro could do nothing but wait for a ride to get them.

Toshiro wanted to scream at all of them. He didn't want tea and scones. *Where the fuck are my sodding husband and sister?*

"How long do we have to wait for a ride?" Dom crushed the paper cup of tea, sloshing the hot liquid everywhere. She dropped it instantly to the ground and had to hunt for napkins to clean up the mess. "*Shit.*"

"Too long." Toshiro checked his watch. "Hope the bastards didn't destroy our phones. I hate having to get a new one."

"Priorities, Tosh."

He rubbed absently at a black smudge on his finger that he'd gotten at some point in the boot. "If I think about it, I'll lose my fucking mind, Dom. I can't do it. Can't live in a world without my husband or my twin in it. Can't bloody well do it."

Dom budged over to lean against the wall next to him. "What's wrong with a new phone?"

"Nothing. *Everything.*" Toshiro glanced up when an unmarked SUV pulled up inches from them. "Our chariot awaits."

And here's hoping so do Charlie and Mack.

CHAPTER THIRTY-ONE

MACK

They sat on a brick wall not far from the stable with a blanket stretched around them. The house had freaked Charlie out, so they'd decided not to stay inside. Mack had done a quick wash up to get most of the gunge off his clothes and hands, enough he no longer offended Charlie's extremely sensitive sense of smell.

The blanket had been filched from the back of a sofa. They hadn't managed to reach Seeta, and wanted to avoid calling Jude. Mack had no idea if Rafe had the ability to trace the calls and refused to risk Jude's safety.

He eventually got hold of one of the detectives at the surgery where Pierce was recuperating. The man promised to contact Seeta with their location. They'd nothing left to do but wait for help—or daylight, when Mack could then perhaps see his way to driving to safety—if the car was still there.

Beside him on the wall, Charlie had huddled into herself.

She'd gone silent ten minutes into waiting for rescue. Mack couldn't do much for her aside from not pressing her; when she went nonverbal, forcing her to try to speak did nothing other than exacerbate the situation.

Darkness slowly gave way to light, and Mack thought it might be around five in the morning. The sun had started to make its presence known. A tiny part of the tension in his body dissipated with his ability to see returning—only a small bit, though, with so much up in the air.

"Did you hear that?"

Mack glanced over at Charlie, who'd jumped off the wall. "Hear what?"

"Shhh." She waved her hand frantically at him and tilted her head slightly as if trying to hear better. "I heard a car."

Mack climbed up on the wall to attempt to see over the small rise in the path leading towards the main house and front gate. "Are you sure?"

Charlie narrowed her eyes at him. "Yes, I'm sure. I heard tires on gravel. It's distinctive."

A minute later, her incredible hearing was proven correct. Two blacked-out SUVs drove down the path towards them. Mack tensed when they slowed to a stop but relaxed when Seeta Joseph climbed out of one of them.

What does Jude always say?

Right.

The cavalry has arrived.

"Toshi—"

Seeta brought a hand up to stop him. She had her phone to one ear. "I've got them both here safe. Hold on a second."

Mack easily caught the phone tossed to him. "Hello?"

"Oh my fucking God. Gregor?"

Mack collapsed back on the wall, relief taking his breath away. He clutched the phone without being able to really process. Hearing Toshiro's voice, so clearly alive and well, sent a wave of emotion through him. "Tosh?"

"Gregor." Toshiro sounded as if his throat had clogged up. "You all right? Charlie? Is she fine?"

Mack tugged Charlie into his arms. She'd started crying at hearing her brother's voice on speaker phone. "We're cold, bit stinky, but mostly good."

"He's got a concussion and was covered in cow shit," Charlie offered helpfully. "He still stinks a bit."

"A concussion?"

"I'm fine, Tosh. I promise. Just want to see you." Mack left off that he also had a serious need to visit pain and suffering upon Rafe and his little gang of idiots. "Where are you?"

"On the way to you. Think we're an hour out." Toshiro cleared his throat loudly. "Why'd they leave you two and take us?"

"I've no bloody clue." Mack noticed Seeta trying to discreetly get his attention. "Think our detective wants her mobile back. See you in a bit. Tosh?"

"Hmm?"

"Love you."

Toshiro cleared his throat for the second time. "I love you as well, *amor*."

The hour dragged on far longer than the night had done.

Mack didn't hear a word of what Seeta said to him. He barely paid attention when his phone and wallet were returned to him; it seemed they'd been left in the lodge.

"They're fine. We picked them up from the petrol station, and both appeared completely unharmed." Seeta tried to ease his worry. "We managed to get the identity of the two men in the BMW they were taken in. Both are actually known to the police; they've connections with an Eastern European arms dealer we've been investigating for a few years. We've never managed to connect him to a specific country or even identify him by anything other than a nickname."

Mack exchanged a glance with Charlie when she mentioned the arms dealer. He wondered if perhaps it had all been connected from the beginning. "While you continue your search of the property, I think we'll wait outside."

Charlie followed him away from the police. "What do we do?"

"Plan. Carefully, this time." Mack sent a few texts to Jude, warning him to be careful and to send a friend over to check on Toshiro's mother. She'd be a soft target for Rafe when he realised his rabbits had escaped the snare. "They won't get away with this."

And by they, I mostly mean Rafe.

I'll gut the sodding bastard.

Charlie offered Mentos to him. "One of the lovely police gave them to me. They didn't have a snack. I'm starved."

"We'll find something." Mack had no doubts Toshiro or Dom would've made sure to grab a snack for Charlie. She didn't do well without frequent meals. "You doing okay?"

"Managing."

Managing.

Charlie-speak for I'm only going to be able to maintain this pretend normalcy for a bit longer. Hurry up, Dom. Of everyone in their circle, Dom knew the ins and outs of helping Charlie when necessary.

"Another motor."

Mack had yet another rush of adrenaline flow through him. He waited, tapping his fingers rapidly against his thigh, watching for a sign of what Charlie could hear. *"C'mon."*

Yet another Range Rover made its way down the path. It barely slowed down before Dom had launched herself out of the back seat. She raced full speed to reach Charlie; the two women fell into each other's arms.

Mack drew away to allow them a bit of privacy. His attention stayed focused on his husband, who'd waited for the SUV to actually stop before getting out. "Tosh."

"Gregor?" His husband stood like a statue. Mack strode quickly towards him. His hands clutched Toshiro's shoulders, holding him still while he looked at him carefully for any sign of injury.

"You're okay. You're *actually* okay." Mack hadn't wanted to believe Seeta or even Toshiro himself. He slid his fingers from his husband's shoulders around to the back of his neck, guiding him forward into his arms. "I couldn't see a bloody thing in the dark. I couldn't…. Fucking helpless and useless. Thought I'd lost you. Not sure I'd manage."

Toshiro slipped icy hands underneath Mack's shirt and borrowed jacket. His fingers gripped him by the sides painfully. "We heard gunshots."

Looping one arm around Toshiro's shoulders, Mack kept his other hand on his husband's neck. He pressed him flush against his body, not wanting to let go again.

Ever.

Toshiro hesitated a second before his arms slipped around Mack. He rested his forehead against his husband's. "Two gunshots. You didn't come back. Neither did Charlie."

Mack played with the silken strands of hair at the base of Toshiro's neck. "Do you know how much I fucking love you?"

"Tosh?" Charlie approached them hesitantly.

Mack reluctantly released his husband to allow the twins to embrace. "Go on, then. I'm going to have a word with our detective friend."

Wonder if they'd let us borrow one of their fancy SUVs?

"Mr—"

"Mack. Just stick with Mack." He cut Seeta off; his eyes couldn't help drifting to Toshiro again. The twins were still clinging to one another, Dom keeping watch nearby. "Have you found anything of interest?"

She turned an apologetic smile towards him, and Mack knew their cooperation had come to an end. "Given the people involved, my superiors feel it best you not insert yourself further into the investigation."

Mack didn't waste any of his anger on her. He knew the detectives wouldn't want the thieves putting their noses in and ruining their case. "Can you give us a lift since they swanned off with my car?"

We'll do some Rafe hunting on our own.

CHAPTER THIRTY-TWO

TOSHIRO

After getting dropped off near their loft, Toshiro led the way up to their place. He wasn't surprised to find Jude waiting anxiously for them. Their home had better security than his flat.

With Mack immediately disappearing into their bedroom to shower, Toshiro was torn. Should he stay to comfort his sister, who seemed to be in shock? Or reconnect with his husband to allay the irrational fears tugging at him?

"I'm sure Mack could use your help. I'll keep an eye on these two." Jude nudged Toshiro with his wheelchair. "Off you go, if you're going to fuck each other, try to keep it down, yeah?"

"*Jude.*"

"We're fine, Tosh." Dom waved him on while she continued to cuddle up with Charlie on the sofa. "We'll start formulating a plan."

"Check Mack's cuts and the contusion on his head,"

Charlie called after him.

Oh, I'll inspect every inch of his body.

Toshiro strode quickly down the hall towards the privacy of their bedroom. He stepped inside to find a naked Mack sitting on the edge of the bed with his head in his hands. "Gregor?"

Closing the door, Toshiro rushed over to kneel in front of him. Mack didn't even look at him. His fingers threaded through his hair, tugging hard on it.

Toshiro reached up to untangle his husband's fingers. "You're too young to go bald."

"I was blind."

"Pardon?" Toshiro sat back on his heels with his hands holding tightly to Mack's. "*Amor?*"

In a heartbreakingly halting speech, Mack unloaded all of his pain and struggle from the previous night. Toshiro felt tears dropping on his hands from his husband's eyes. He patiently waited for him to get everything out—all the agonising frustration at his own limitations.

"Fucking useless."

"Not quite." Toshiro decided his husband had wallowed in pain sufficiently for one day. He refused to allow him to beat himself up over it. "You crawled your way to the stable. You got to Charlie—you got her free and safe. What more could you have done if you'd been able to see perfectly?"

"I don't know." Mack lifted his head up to meet Toshiro's gaze. "I've avoided being out at night as it's gotten worse. In the city, there are so many lights to provide edges to guide me."

"Yet, you managed," Toshiro insisted. He brought a thumb up to brush a tear from his husband's cheek. "You could've stayed in the field."

"With the cow shit?"

Toshiro wrinkled his nose dramatically. "I thought I smelled something."

"You arse." Mack shoved him, which sent Toshiro stumbling onto his back. "I'll have a quick shower."

"Or a long bath?"

"Your idea is better." Mack rubbed his hand across his face with a weary groan. "I'd no idea how to comfort Charlie when we thought you might not be coming back to us."

Toshiro had the lump in his throat again, just imagining how distraught they must've been. He'd been so focused on getting free and his own grief that he hadn't fully considered what Mack and Charlie went through. "We stay together— no matter what. We tackle this together, Gregor."

"Mary, first." Mack pulled himself up off the bed. He reached out to begin to unbutton Toshiro's shirt. "Then Rafe. The arms dealer is out of our scope. We'll allow Seeta to handle it."

Toshiro toed off his shoes and his socks. He waited as Mack moved from his shirt to his jeans and boxers. His husband clearly needed some semblance of normalcy and control. "Cleaning up, first. Then plotting."

Their lovemaking over the years had always held an edge of playfulness to it. Neither Mack or Toshiro ever took anything too seriously, aside from the safety of family and friends. Something had changed in his husband within the last twenty-four hours.

The teasing touches had given way to more methodical caresses. Mack's fingers drifted over every inch of Toshiro's body before they'd even made it into the tub filled with hot sudsy water. It occurred to him that his husband was trying to memorise the way he looked and felt.

Before his sight goes.

Merde.

He watched Mack hop quickly into the shower stall on the other side of the tub to rinse the worst of the crud left on his body. *What must it be like to fear you'll eventually be unable to see the man you love? Could I handle it?*

How do I help him handle it?

"Enjoying the view?" Mack stepped out of the shower still dripping water everywhere. "Fuck. It's freezing. In the tub?"

Toshiro waited until Mack got comfortable then sat in their large garden tub between his legs. He rested his hands on his husband's thighs. "*Sei l'amore grande della mia vita.*"

"I love you too. I'm just not all showy and dramatic about it." Mack slipped his arm around him. He played absently with one of Toshiro's nipple rings. "I don't know the words—but the tone says your heart is mine."

"And you said you're not all showy and dramatic." Toshiro tilted his head to the side to brush his lips against Mack's.

It hit him, suddenly: in the scope of a day, he could've lost his husband. He'd loved Mack almost from day one.

His life didn't work without him.

"Tosh?"

He twisted around in the tub, straddling Mack's legs. Toshiro's fingers gripped his husband by the shoulders. His lips descended into a kiss filled with all the desperate emotions flowing through him.

"I need to be in you," Toshiro growled against Mack's lips. "Have to feel you underneath me."

I have to know you're still alive and well.

Neither fast nor feverishly, the two men languidly enjoyed each other's body. Toshiro wasn't satisfied until they'd used up every ounce of energy after their exhausting evening. He collapsed on top of Mack, dropping his head on his husband's damp chest.

"Toshi." Mack tapped him on the arm. "*Tosh.*"

"What?" He found lifting his head required an exhausting amount of effort. "Something wrong?"

"Water's gone cold—and you're starting to drool on my chest." Mack brought his hands up to slowly lift Toshiro off him. "We also might want to make sure the animals haven't destroyed the living room."

"I'm telling Dom you called her an animal." Toshiro clambered slowly out of the tub. He grabbed a towel to wrap around himself as the cooler air hit him. "Are you as starved as I am?"

Mack snuck a hand out to grab him firmly by the arse. "Not nearly as much as before."

Toshiro thought the bath and sex would settle his emotions. They hadn't, not entirely. "Feeling better?"

Mack stopped drying himself off to motion towards him. "Come here, love."

The tight hug lasted long enough they'd almost dried off just from standing around. Toshiro couldn't bring himself to let Mack go. He pressed his face against his husband's neck, ignoring the way his beard tickled his nose.

"Oi. Will you two hurry up? I made a curry for us." Dom banged loudly on the door. "Also, Jude broke five of your glasses trying to juggle. We cleaned it up."

"You were saying about the animals in the zoo?" Mack released Toshiro with a laugh. He ran his fingers across his husband's chest before stepping away. "Curry. Plotting. And getting Jude to stop trying to juggle because he's shit at it. Can we schedule a nap later?"

He had no doubts they'd all need more than a nap. None of them had truly processed the trauma visited on them. In all their years running jobs, they'd always gone out of their way to avoid weapons and violence.

"So, how are we gutting Rafe the rat?" Jude didn't mince words when he spotted Mack and Toshiro the second they stepped into the living room. "Oh, and I didn't smash the glasses. Dom failed to catch one of the satsumas I was juggling."

"You can't juggle." Toshiro pinched the bridge of his nose while Dom and Mack both cackled with laughter. His twin giggled in the corner where she'd sat down with a cup of tea. "You can't. You keep trying, but you fail."

"I thought sex was supposed to improve your mood?" Jude swerved his wheelchair out of the way of Toshiro's kick.

"I'll report you to adult services."

"All right, children, play nice." Mack stepped in while Toshiro let loose a string of Japanese swearing that would've made his grandfather proud. "Where's this curry?"

"In the pot." Dom knocked the side of it with the wooden spoon in her hand. "So, not to dwell on the nasty bits, but how are we kicking Rafe in the stones?"

"Cut 'em off," Charlie interjected.

"His stones?" Toshiro winced at the idea then decided perhaps Rafe had brought it on himself. "First we have to find them—him and Mary, not his bollocks. Any suggestions?"

CHAPTER THIRTY-THREE

MACK

Several days later, they'd made little progress aside from a bit of spying. Mack's patience was being sorely tested. He wanted revenge—and an end to the nightmare.

"If you say we're on a witch hunt one more sodding time, I will think of something terrible to do to you." Toshiro shoved Mack, almost sending him toppling off the railing they'd perched themselves on. "Keep it together, will you?"

Mack reached over to tweak Toshiro's nipple through his shirt and tugged on the ring in it as retaliation. "She's a witch. And we're hunting for her."

"She's not *actually* a witch." Toshiro flicked him on the nose.

Mack rubbed his nose a few times before pinching it to stop the sneeze. "Wanker. Tell Charlie to stop infecting you with her verbal pedantism."

"In fairness, I do it to bug the shit out of you. Charlie does it because she believes it's important to be precise and

clear when speaking. No messing around with your words."
Toshiro shifted to lean against the wall. "Why did we decide
the roof was the best place for this?"

"We didn't." Mack had argued with Dom and Jude
about the safest place to stalk the first of their prey. They
all believed Mary would be far easier to get a hold of than
Rafe. She might lead them to him, though. "Your sister's
girlfriend decided the tallest and heaviest members of our
group should climb up onto a roof to watch the witch's flat."

Well, technically, we aren't on a roof.

They'd found a penthouse apartment with a terrace
looking over Mary's building. Toshiro talked their way
inside. Mack knew they had a limited amount of time; they
were just waiting for Jude to tell them the cameras they'd
sneakily put up worked.

"What is taking so sodding long?" Mack hopped off the
railing. He knew they couldn't hang out indefinitely at the
penthouse.

"Call him."

Mack grabbed his phone, quickly dialling Jude. "He's
not answering."

"Try Dom."

"She's not answering either." Mack had a sudden,
terrifying sense of déjà vu. "Neither is Charlie."

"Charlie always answers when it's you or me." Toshiro
grabbed his jacket from the railing and strode over to him.
"Let's go. Cameras are up. If they're not working, nothing
we can do about it now."

They raced to their loft. Mack froze at the sight of the

open front door. *Fuck.*

He expected the worst when he got inside—not to find Jude, Charlie, and Dom laughing, albeit a little hysterically, at a bound Mary Shipton who sat on the sofa.

Jude grinned at the two out-of-breath men, throwing a cricket ball up in the air repeatedly. "Turns out, I don't need legs to kick arse. I'm fucking brilliant. Worship at the altar of my magnificence."

"How many pints have you had this morning?" Mack easily caught the cricket ball flung at him. "Wasn't this in our bedroom?"

At school, Mack had preferred rugby to other sports. Toshiro had been a gifted cricket player. He'd even travelled with an under-21 team for a year; the ball Jude tossed over was a souvenir from his husband's last game.

"Is that a pistol?" Toshiro drew his attention to the weapon sticking out from under the armchair across from their sofa. "What the hell happened?"

"Don't touch it," Charlie shouted when Mack crouched down to pick it up. "She brought it."

"We called Seeta," Dom added helpfully.

"Again, I say, what the bloody hell happened?" Toshiro grabbed Mack by the shirt to drag him away when he started towards Mary. "Keep your temper, *amor.*"

Mack sneered at the bound woman who glared silently at all of them. "How's it feel to be trussed up? Maybe we should find a field to dump you in—see how you enjoy it."

"Gregor." Toshiro rested his hand against Mack's neck. His fingers rubbed his tense muscles. "Easy does it. She's not worth it."

Mack didn't necessarily agree. He thought giving her a taste of his suffering would be worth it. "Fine."

The others evidently decided a distraction might be useful. Jude manoeuvred his wheelchair forward to block their view of Mary. He explained how they'd briefly heard the alarm trigger before she'd stepped in with a gun pointed at Charlie's head.

Both Mack and Toshiro immediately glanced towards Charlie; she smiled briefly but returned to the Rubik's Cube in her hands. She twisted it around to match the colours up. Jude continued on with his story.

"I'm a fucking cricket god."

"What the hell are you on about?" Mack drew his attention away from scowling hatefully at their captive to Jude, who pointed towards the cricket ball. "You didn't."

"I did." Jude stretched his arm out to pat himself on the back. "Best throw I've ever made in cricket."

"We impressed upon the bitch her mistake in taking Charlie as the weakest link in our group." Dom had one arm wrapped possessively around her girlfriend. "She kicked her arse."

"I did." Charlie didn't even glance up from her twisting and turning of the Rubik's Cube. "Also, she smells."

"Good or bad?" Mack couldn't help the question even though Toshiro whacked him on the stomach for it. "What?"

A knock on the door interrupted their joking around. Toshiro disappeared down the hall, returning moments later with Seeta and two other detectives. She shook her head in disbelief when she spotted Mary.

"Weren't you supposed to stay out of it?" Seeta asked pointedly.

"I've a video of what happened." Jude held up a thumb drive. "Want it? We didn't invite her to break in and point a gun at Charlie's head."

Mack intended to add his own thoughts, but a buzz from his phone interrupted. "We're a bit busy, Nico."

"Think you'll want to hear this, Mack-n-cheese," Nico replied. "One of my clients slipped a bit of information to me about someone you might be looking for."

"Thought you had a policy of staying out of shit?" Mack had never expected Nico to involve himself. They'd helped him, but a fence only kept his worth by respecting the privacy of all of his clients. "Don't risk yourself for us."

"You don't try to kill my friends. Hang on." Nico yelled something that Mack couldn't quite understand. He figured his friend had covered his phone with his hand. "Sorry. Rafe's on his way to Istanbul, again. He's meeting with one of his contacts. I'd bet my entire fucking bank account he's left Mary to take the fall for him. Texting Jude the information. Don't get your arses killed."

"Just our arses?" Mack chuckled. He laughed again when he realised Nico had hung up on him. "Cheeky fucking bastard."

"Problem?"

Mack shook his head at Toshiro. He calmly stepped into the argument happening between Jude, Dom, and the detective. "We do apologise, Detective Joseph. If we'd known Ms Shipton intended to assault us, I'm confident Jude, Dom, or Charlie would immediately have contacted you. The video, the weapon, and the witch are all yours. I hope it makes for quite the feather in your career. Good luck capturing both Elwyn and Bishop."

With a perfectly polite smile, Mack guided all of the police out of the loft. He twisted around to make a face at Toshiro, who only rolled his eyes. *Everyone's a critic.* They all breathed a bit easier once the detectives had gone.

"One down. Two to go?" Charlie set her completed Rubik's Cube to one side. She eased out of Dom's arms to give her brother a hug. "She smelled weird."

Mack stepped around the twins over to Jude, who'd wheeled himself over to the windows on the other side of the room. "Nico messaged you the information. Take a look, will you?"

"I saved us." Jude didn't acknowledge Mack's question at all. "I did it."

"Of course you did. You're completely capable of doing anything you set your mind to—except maybe wanking." Mack grunted when Jude punched him in the stomach. "You've never been useless."

"Right."

Mack knew his friend had never wanted pity. He even chafed when offered help of any kind. They'd worked hard to support Jude however he needed them. "How's the toe?"

"Doc thinks it was a phantom sensation." Jude shrugged. "How's the sight?"

"I crawled through cow shit because I couldn't see a

fucking thing." Mack knew that in Jude he had someone who completely understood the fears that came with losing a basic ability. "So, we're not perfect, but we're managing it. We're capable."

"We are." Jude scrubbed a hand roughly across his face, and Mack kindly pretended not to see it. "What's this about Nico?"

CHAPTER THIRTY-FOUR

TOSHIRO

Sitting on the floor by the windows, Toshiro stared up at the sliver of a moon barely visible through the haze of clouds. He sat with his back to the side of the sofa and his knees bent up. A glass of wine dangled loosely from his fingers.

Dom and Charlie had left after lunch to spend time at his mum's. The two would keep an eye on her. Toshiro wouldn't put it past Rafe to strike out at their extended circle, as his attempts to hurt them directly had failed twice.

It took a bit of arguing, but Jude had agreed to spend a few days with some old schoolmates who happened to be retired Royal Marines. Toshiro pitied anyone who struck out with the men around. He'd seen them in action a few times.

"Tosh?"

He didn't really register Mack until his husband had crouched in front of him to lift the glass out of his hand. "Did I wake you?"

"Missed your snoring."

"Impressed you managed the walk from the bedroom to here without tripping." Toshiro gave a half-hearted chuckle.

"I could walk through our flat with my eyes shut," Mack said confidently.

Except you can't, love. Not consistently, as proved when you practised with the safe.

"How many times have you practised?" His heart clenched painfully when his husband admitted to walking through their loft with his eyes closed during the day to prepare for the inevitable. He knew they couldn't continue to lie to themselves, but pushing Mack might not help either. "*Gregor.*"

"Leave it." Mack put the glass on the nearby coffee table then took a seat in front of him. He stretched his legs out on either side of him while his hands rested on Toshiro's knees. "What's keeping you up, love?"

"The game changed on us." Toshiro had struggled to keep the vision of the pistol pressed against his sister's head out of his mind. "It's gotten life-threateningly dangerous."

Mack tilted his head to the side. His hands caressed Toshiro gently. "Not sure it's ever been anything other than walking along the knife edge of danger. We just blissfully ignored it. We were addicted to the adrenaline rush of getting one over on people."

"We've never been left for dead, or thrown in the boot of a car, or threatened with death." Toshiro hadn't necessarily looked on their lives with rose-tinted glasses, but looking back he thought they'd all been foolishly glib about the dangers. "Your father's in jail, your uncle's in critical condition, Charlie had a gun to her head; when does it end? What's the climax of all this drama caused by Rafe? We're perilously close to losing everything, Gregor. And for what? The greed of a wannabe Prince John?"

"Okay. I love you with all my heart. But you're beginning to sound a bit obsessed with this whole Robin Hood thing." Mack easily deflected his half-hearted kick. "Besides, he's more the Sherriff of Nottingham than the prince."

"Still an evil fucking bastard." Toshiro shuffled forward until he could wrap himself around his husband. "We can't follow him from country to country. One, we don't have the wealth he has to throw around. Two, he'd be at an advantage with his contacts already there. Three, I don't have a third one yet."

"Three, you're worried we'll take unnecessary risks again with it only being the two of us." Mack shifted his legs wider open to allow Toshiro to slide even closer to him. "You're scared."

"They held a gun to Charlie's head. You got pistol whipped. Of course, I'm sodding afraid." He made himself take a few deep breaths. The last thing they needed was to go off at each other. "Sorry."

"Don't. It's a shit situation. I'm surprised none of us flipped out on Shipton. Should've let Dom go at her for a bit." Mack traced one of the scars on Toshiro's knees. "Do we walk away?"

"Not sure there's a witness protection program for thieves." Toshiro grabbed his glass to get another sip, then offered it to Mack. "We've ruined this for Rafe. He's not the type to let it go. Even if we never interfered with him ever again, he holds grudges. Look at your dad. Look at what happened to Pierce."

"Hmm." Mack turned his head to the side, obviously wanting to avoid the subject.

"Gregor." He covered his husband's hands resting on his knees. "It's not your fault."

"I know that."

Toshiro found it hard to believe when Mack couldn't even meet his gaze. "It's late."

"I'm aware."

Pushing up on Mack's legs, Toshiro used them as leverage to get to his feet. He pulled his husband up with him. They stumbled down the hall to the bedroom, collapsing on the bed with tired groans.

The problem of dealing with Trev and Rafe could wait.

We keep putting off all these problems. Mack's sight. Rafe. We're starting to run out of time.

CHAPTER THIRTY-FIVE

MACK

"Your husband will kill you in the most torturous fashion possible when he realises what you're doing." Nico jogged beside him to keep up with his longer stride. "*Oi.* Mack-n-cheese. Are you listening to me?"

"I am not actually listening to you." Mack had left Toshiro in bed asleep after being unable to sleep himself. He'd dressed quickly, called Nico to meet up with him, and headed out once it had gotten light enough for him to be able to see. "What are you whinging about now?"

"Toshiro. Death. Pain."

"Right." Mack stretched an arm out to muss up Nico's hair. "I'm not doing anything dangerous—yet."

He wasn't. His idea had evolved from idiotically risky to only mildly so. If it all came off brilliantly, Toshiro wouldn't have any reason to be hacked off at him.

"And waltzing into Scotland Yard is what?"

"A calculated plan." He wanted to dismantle the support

system around Rafe. They'd gotten Shipton out of the way, now he wanted to ensure Elwyn didn't escape either. "Jude's going to help me ensure we get into Seeta's computer safely."

"Surrounded by the police?" Nico grabbed his arm to slow him down. "What's the rush? It's not even eight in the morning."

"Yes, Gregor. What is the rush?"

Mack spun around to find a breathless Toshiro a few feet behind them. "Bugger."

Nico glanced between the two of them a few times, patted Mack on the arm, and began to walk away. "Good luck."

Offering Toshiro a wry grin, Mack attempted to charm his way out of an argument. Of all the places in London, surely the New Scotland Yard building was one of the safest. Trev Elywn had been outed as a dirty cop; the odds of running into either him or Rafe were slim to none.

"And getting caught tampering with a detective sergeant's computer?" Toshiro looped his arm around Mack's, forcibly guiding him in the opposite direction. "Clever idea, dreadful plan."

"Everyone's a critic," Mack grumbled. "Jude did try to talk me out of it."

"Why don't we grab a coffee and come up with a better plan?" Toshiro snickered at him as they crossed the street. "Stop pouting. It's not nearly as adorable as you think."

"*Rude.*" Mack yanked him out of the street a second later when a cab whipped by them. "What an arse."

They found a nearby café to grab coffees and a few breakfast pastries, then wandered across the street to a small park. Mack hadn't bothered to eat before he'd left the flat. He didn't know how Toshiro had caught up with him so quickly, though he wondered if Nico had ratted him out—or Jude.

His plan hadn't been totally daft. Getting to Trev required more information than they had. Jude hadn't found any digital trail to follow on the man.

"If Elwyn has any sense at all, he's gone off the grid. He knows Interpol and CID are after him. Only a fool would prance around without any precautions. He might've already left the country. Do we know for certain he's not with Rafe?" Toshiro tossed a piece of his pastry at a group of nearby birds. "Maybe they believe in safety in numbers?"

"With Rafe?" Mack shook his head. His mentor had shown himself to be incapable of showing loyalty to anyone. "I got a text early, by the way. Uncle Pierce is awake."

"Going to visit?"

"Maybe." Mack tried to go for indifference, but his voice shook slightly. "Yes."

"Why don't you drive up to see him in the hospital? I've a visit of my own to make." Toshiro crumpled up the paper bag, shoving it into the pocket of his jacket. "I made an appointment with the prison to see your father."

"What?"

"He won't talk to you about whatever happened so many years ago. Maybe he's afraid of what you'll think of him?" Toshiro glanced at his watch. "Dom's going to give me a lift up since Charlie doesn't want to leave Mum alone right now."

"When are you getting your license?"

"As if I have time to worry about that nonsense with all this going on?" Toshiro canted his head to rest it against Mack's shoulder. "I've only one more lesson to go before I try to get my license. You'll be pleased to know Nico's already arranging for a new vehicle for you. Should be here in a few minutes so you can go see your uncle."

"You are all sneaky and conniving traitors." Mack glared at Toshiro when his husband snickered at him. "You're supposed to be on my side."

"I'm on the side of you not doing something idiotic." He leaned over to brush his lips against the side of Mack's downturned mouth. "We've got to be extra careful now, *amor*. They're not playing fair."

Dom arrived not long after to take Toshiro away. Mack cursed himself for getting distracted from getting to the bottom of what he planned to ask his dad. *I'm supposed to be the smooth-talking bastard. Damn it.*

A little over two hours later, Mack found himself staring at the entryway to his uncle's hospital room. He ignored the two police playing guard dog on either side of it. One of the officers cleared his throat loudly before reaching over to open the door for him.

Arsehole.

All through the drive, Mack had gone over in his mind how to approach his uncle. He didn't want to pepper an injured man with questions, but who else could provide answers? His father wasn't likely to confess anything to Toshiro, no matter how confident his husband might be.

Even with the door now swung open, Mack hesitated to cross the threshold. He glared at the cop who chuckled at him. His legs didn't seem to want to move forward no matter how hard he tried.

"Going to come in or should they help you walk as well?" Pierce teased hoarsely. He appeared incredibly pale outside of the many bruises, but awake and clearheaded. "Take a seat, Mack. I'm too weak to bite. And I'd say we have quite a bit to discuss, don't we?"

Mack walked inside, closing the door behind him and sitting in the chair next to the bed. "Do we?"

"Hope you enjoy stories." Pierce grabbed the cup of water sitting on the tray on his lap. "Even if it's not a pretty one."

CHAPTER THIRTY-SIX

With Dom waiting outside for him, Toshiro made his way through the security checks to get into the prison. He found himself led to a room where his father-in-law joined him after a few minutes. The man had gotten significantly frailer than the last time he'd seen him.

"Did my son send you?" He lowered himself into one of the chairs at the square table in the centre of the room that one of the guards guided him over to. "It's been years since you visited."

"It was more important for Mack to see you." Toshiro had never wanted to take the one visit allowed to his father-in-law. "I—"

"Stop." His father-in-law held his hand up to cut him off. "You want to know about Rafe Bishop."

Settling into his own seat, Toshiro nodded in response. Mack's approach usually tended to arguing someone into answering. He preferred to draw them out with silence.

"Your old man used to watch me like that." He stared in Toshiro's general direction. "I can feel the weight of your silence even if I can't see more than a fuzzy image of you."

Toshiro blinked at him in total shock. "You knew my father?"

"Ran in the same circles. A long time ago. Another casualty of Rafe's greed." Gregor, the senior, smiled at him. "We all knew each other. Part of the same crew in some ways, not as close as your little group."

All of his carefully crafted questions flew out of his mind. Toshiro's mum had gone out of her way to avoid telling them much about their father. He'd known only bits and pieces from letters and family rumours.

Toshiro compartmentalised his thoughts; he couldn't allow himself to be distracted by the carrot of information being dangled in front of him. "Tell me about Rafe."

"You never were controlled by your emotions like my son." He coughed violently and leaned wearily into the uncomfortable steel chair. "How's his sight? He never tells me the truth about it. Just says not to worry, as if I've anything better to do with my time in here."

"Worsening." Toshiro respected his father-in-law enough to speak the truth. "He's struggling to adapt—to accept the reality of it."

"He's an Easton. We don't accept. We fight." He gave a hoarse laugh and lifted his shackled hands. "I used to be that way."

"What happened?" Toshiro asked, unable to stop himself from posing the question. "What changed? Why've you never really fought for your innocence to be free?"

"My son's life." His eyes suddenly held a fierce strength that reminded Toshiro of his husband. "What would you sacrifice for him? For your twin? Is your freedom worth their safety?"

"I'd sacrifice everything for him. *Every-fucking-thing.*" Toshiro felt a few of the puzzle pieces fall into place for him. "Rafe threatened Mack. You played the patsy on purpose. Why didn't you ever tell us? We could've—"

"Nothing you did would've changed the situation." He coughed again, worse than the first time. "Rafe promised to leave Mack alone. It kept me silent even with my health deteriorating. And besides, who'd believe me now? Every man in here protests their innocence. I'd be just another liar in a sea of them."

Toshiro ignored the tutting from the guard and reached across the table to take his father-in-law's hands in his own. "He won't get away with this."

"He'll kill you if you get in his way."

"Time's up." The prison guard did offer Toshiro an apologetic smile that seemed more grimace than anything else. "You've had your chat."

Without bothering to say goodbye, his father-in-law allowed himself to be led from the room. Toshiro exited the prison in a bit of a fog. Dom watched him walking towards her with a worried frown on her face.

"Tosh?" she asked once he'd practically fallen into the car seat. "Want to talk about it?"

"Not yet."

The first hour of the drive went by in almost complete silence. Toshiro wished there'd been more time to talk about not only Rafe, but his own father. He wondered how many unexplained problems in their lives could actually be placed at Rafe's feet.

"Tosh?"

He glanced up when Dom whacked him on the arm "What?"

"Think the silver Range Rover is following us." She glanced into her rear-view mirror. "It's the one about two cars behind us. I've switched lanes three times, and it follows a few seconds after."

Toshiro sat up in the seat and tried to subtly peek behind to catch a view of it. "Can't see the driver."

"I can't say for certain, but I believe they got on the motorway with us as well." Dom switched lanes once again. Her eyes darted up to the mirror. "And they've followed again. Whoever it is has obviously never learnt how to be subtle while stalking someone."

"Or they want us to know they're there."

"Shit. That's even worse." She tapped her fingers absently against the steering wheel. "Do we continue on to London as if they're not there? Try to shake them?"

"Easier to shake them in the city." Toshiro wanted the identity of the driver but didn't want to risk a confrontation. "If they followed us from the prison, someone's been watching it to see if Mack visited his father. How else would they know?"

"Tracking our phones?"

"Jude ensured that wasn't possible." Toshiro had made certain their technologically savvy friend checked all of their mobiles after the attempted kidnapping. "It has to be Rafe—or one of his hired help. He knows Mack well enough to know he'd reach out to his father for information."

"What do we do?" Dom continued to skilfully weave in and out of traffic. She sped up slightly, then slowed down while they both watched to see what the Range Rover would do. "Still following."

"We've two options: continue on to London or force the issue by exiting at the next service station to see if they follow." Toshiro hadn't decided what they'd do if forced into a confrontation. "Mack's at the hospital, so I don't want to disturb him."

And what can he do from near Aylesbury anyway?

"I'm pulling off the motorway." Dom made the decision for both of them. "Not letting these wankers screw around with us any longer."

"Pun intended?"

Dom's glare told him precisely what she thought of his attempt to lighten the mood. "If the petrol station isn't busy enough, I'll drive on to the next one. I'm not risking them trying something without witnesses."

It surprised neither of them when minutes after they parked in front of the service station, the Range Rover made its way over to one of the pumps. Toshiro watched surreptitiously while pretending to check the engine of their vehicle. He got his first clear view of the driver—Trev Elywn.

Well, hello there, Mr Corrupt Detective Inspector, fancy meeting you here.

How utterly random to see you at the same service station?

Dom joined him at the front of the car; she bent forward as if to inspect the engine with him. "Seeta Joseph said to try to drive as slowly as humanly possible, stopping at every service station. She's getting a team together to take Elywn down."

"You called her?" Toshiro had a hard time believing Dom had voluntarily reached out to Seeta. Of all their group, she tended to be the most vocal about police involvement in their lives. "Shocking."

"Don't be a twat." She shoved him hard on the shoulder. "Time to quit pretending like you understand engines. I've no doubts CID and Interpol are using CCTV to track us on the motorway, so let's get this show on the road. Shall we? I'd prefer to get their eyes off us as soon as possible."

Shutting the bonnet, Toshiro pushed Dom towards the driver side of the vehicle. He had serious doubts about this plan of trying to prolong the chase. Trev hadn't struck him as a complete idiot; he'd eventually twig on to their odd behaviour.

"We'd better hope Seeta manages to get her shit together quickly. I'd rather not drive like my grandmother down the motorway for too long." Dom spent time checking all of her mirrors. She eventually started the vehicle to back out of the parking spot. "The game is afoot."

"You watch too much Sherlock." He easily blocked her

attempt to punch him in the arm. "Violence is never the answer."

"Fuck off."

Toshiro grinned at her then twisted in the seat to watch. "And our audience of one has followed us."

The number of vehicles racing past them while honking and flipping them off was hysterical. Toshiro and Dom made a show of waving at each one. He didn't understand how Trev continued to follow them.

"Did we underestimate his intelligence? He has to realise we know he's there." Toshiro canted the rear-view mirror to get a better view. "I mean, honestly, what's he doing?"

"Trying for the stupidest detective of the year award?" She sped up a little to move better with traffic. They'd hit two jams on the way to London thus far, which worked in their favour. "Has Seeta texted yet?"

"Have you heard a beep?"

To his immense relief, they hit yet another block of bad traffic. An accident had blocked up two lanes ahead of them. Toshiro hoped it lasted long enough to allow for the non-corrupt police to catch up with Elwyn.

Twenty minutes later, Dom's phone did beep. Seeta informed them to hold tight. They had a helicopter overhead keeping an eye on things, using the accident as a cover for its presence.

"Fingers crossed." Dom held both of her hands up with her index and forefingers twisted together. "Two of our problems solved without us having to get involved."

"Kidnapping? Concussions? Slow-speed car chases? We

got dragged into enough as it was." Toshiro tried to breathe through an uncharacteristic bout of anxiety. He hated how their experience had had a lasting effect. "Keep an eye on him. Don't want him trying to make a run for us or for escape."

"Stop being such a worrywart. It'll be fine." Dom sounded far more confident than he felt. She twisted around suddenly to watch through the back window. "The net's tightening on him."

Toshiro watched with her as uniformed detectives converged on Elwyn's vehicle from every angle with the helicopter continuing to hover above as well. "Well, that's done."

"Bit anticlimactic."

"Are you serious? After everything?"

"I wanted them to have to shoot the bastard." Dom turned back around when horns started. She drove forward with traffic. "He's not our problem anymore."

"No." Toshiro couldn't help thinking they'd saved the worst of their problems for last. "Rafe won't go quite so easily."

CHAPTER THIRTY-SEVEN

MACK

The conversation with his uncle had drained Mack. He'd slouched in the seat beside Pierce to attempt to doze for a bit while the man napped. The nurse had come in to berate them for talking for so long.

"He needs his rest."

Well, I sodding need him to answer my bloody questions.

In the end, Mack hadn't shouted at the nurse. He'd allowed his uncle to drift off while he stayed at his side. He planned to wait until Toshiro returned to London before heading home.

The text with a picture of Elwyn's arrest cheered him up immensely. Toshiro explained how it happened. Mack wondered what Rafe intended by having the former detective follow them so obviously.

"How touching, the nephew visiting his uncle in hospital. I might actually sick up." Rafe casually pointed a pistol at Mack when he jolted out of his chair. "What did I tell you about napping on the job? It's always hazardous to your health. Now sit back down."

Shit.

Where the fucking fuck are the police?

Or the nurse?

Or anyone?

Mack sat gingerly in the seat, mind racing to come up with a plan, anything really, to combat the imminent threat in front of him. He only had a penknife in his pocket—sharp, but one didn't bring a knife to a gun fight. "How'd you avoid the nursing staff and the police?"

"Talent."

Mack rolled his eyes at the amount of arrogance dripping from the single world. "Did you kill them?"

"I'd never touch an innocent." Rafe leaned casually against the closed door. "I value life far too much."

Mack barked out a bitter laugh. "What a crock of shit. How many innocent lives has your avarice ruined?"

"None that matter." He shrugged with an air of indifference. "I once believe you to be the perfect apprentice. You're such an abysmal failure to me. How much time and wisdom did I waste on training you to be the perfect thief and conman?"

"None. You scheming, lying, waste of space of a human being wanker." Mack calmly slipped his hands into his trouser pockets. He fingered the pen knife and considered his options. "What's your big plan, Rafe? Hmm? Shoot us both? Even if you've distracted everyone in the building, they'll hear two gunshots."

"Shooting you would be such an inelegant end to your existence. No, I've a much more poetic way to rid myself of your pestilence. It's why I stayed my hand when I could've killed all of you. Such a pleasure to see your fear and helplessness. A pity I never got the chance to play with Dominica and Toshiro. I had such plans for all of you that you almost ruined." Rafe lifted a capped syringe out of his pocket. "You'll inject air into your uncle's bloodstream. Do you think they'll give you a cell next to your father? How lovely to have both Eastons locked up together side by side for the rest of their lives."

Talk.

Do something.

Distract the bastard until you come up with a plan—or help arrives.

We're so fucked.

"That's your grand plan?" Mack inserted as much derision as possible into his voice. "Aren't you tired of playing the same tune? I'd honestly expected something far more imaginative from you. How many times will you write the same story?"

"Why mess with a good thing? Your father, Toshiro's father, Mary, and even Elywn. They all played their parts, and then capitulated, in the end, to allow me to walk away free to pursue other jobs." Rafe sounded inordinately pleased with himself and the blatant destruction of so many lives. "Now, be a good lad and kill your uncle for me."

Where's Tosh when I need his ability to curse in multiple languages? I don't have the right words to eviscerate this piece of shit. What the fuck am I going to do?

Not panic.

That's what I'm going to do.

Because panic never helps anything.

"Done with your inner monologue?" Rafe tapped the pistol against the wall behind him to get Mack's attention. "I'm on a schedule. You'll take this syringe and do what I've told you. Or I'll put a bullet in both your heads. Quit wasting my time."

"Why? Why do this? I've never interfered with your heists." Mack tried one last desperate attempt to gain a bit more time. "If you'd left well enough alone, I'd never have even known about your involvement in any of this."

"Interpol and CID with your uncle at the head delved too close to discovering my involvement in the theft of antiquities. I decided to kill several birds with one stone. It was so easy to lead you by the nose." Rafe took a step towards him, holding the syringe out. "You've all been so dreadfully predictable. You stole the bracelet, as I knew you would, which allowed me to keep track of you for a bit, until you offloaded it. Did you spot the GPS chip in it? How idiotic were you to waltz into my estate? What did you expect me to do? You managed to escape, blind as you are. Still, this wraps things up even nicer. We've all come full circle."

"You ageing, wrinkled, greedy bastard." Mack wanted to dive for the man, but he knew his reaction had to be carefully managed or Toshiro would be burying him. *Shit. Think positive. This isn't the end.* "You disgust me. How could you betray my dad—me like this?"

"Oh, do grow up, Gregor. You've built this image of yourself. We're villains. We're the bad guys. This fairy tale you've made up to feel better about your actions is false. You're no better than I." Rafe took yet another step closer to him, just out of arms reach. "You've always lied to yourself."

"I am *nothing* like you," Mack spat at him. He'd caught movement out of the corner of his eye. Pierce had to be at least aware of the situation. "One day you'll find yourself skewered on your own sword. Or, in simpler terms, go fuck yourself."

"I've grown tired of our conversation." Rafe calmly raised his pistol to point directly at Mack's forehead. His other hand pointedly offered the syringe to him. "I've played enough, Gregor."

Time had run out.

As if orchestrated perfectly, Pierce groaned exaggeratedly to his right. It allowed Mack to sneak his hand out of his pocket with the pocketknife opened. If he could injure Rafe's dominant arm, get the gun out of play, they had a chance.

"Ahh, I did hope Siddall would be awake to watch as you kill him."

The pleasure in Rafe's voice shook Mack. He'd known the man was twisted, but the level of sadistic joy made it hard to stay focused.

"Still jealous of how my sister would never give you the time of day after she met Mack's father?" Pierce apparently knew one of Rafe's sore spots that Mack'd never known existed. "Is that why you mentored my nephew? The son you wanted to be yours?"

"Be *quiet*." Rafe turned to Pierce as his face turned a mottled shade of red. "Shut up. You don't know—"

With Rafe suitably distracted, Mack launched himself out of the chair. He brought the knife up as his former mentor turned to face him. The gun went off as the two men collided; Mack's weapon dug straight into the inside of Rafe's upper arm.

"Mack?" Pierce's shout sounded a million miles away. "Mack? Hang on. I've called for help."

He blinked up at his uncle while his vision started to blur. "I feel so strange."

"Mack?"

CHAPTER THIRTY-NINE

TOSHIRO

"I don't think shouting at Pierce and the doctor in Japanese is going to solve anything." Dom placed a hand on Toshiro's shoulder, trying to calm him down. "I know you want answers, but they can't give them when you're bellowing in five different languages."

Toshiro drew himself up, breathed in and out deeply, and tried to appear at least moderately pleasant. "Where the fuck is my husband?"

Okay, maybe not pleasant, but it was in English.

"*Tosh.*" Dom elbowed him in the side.

"If you're both done, perhaps I can tell you what happened?" Pierce interrupted.

Between the doctor and Pierce, they explained Rafe's attack along with the fallout from it. Mack had been shot in the leg while trying to disarm him. In the process, he'd stabbed his former mentor in the arm.

"He nicked an artery in Rafe's upper arm. They tried

to stop the bleeding but failed." Pierce didn't appear too broken up about it. "Mack's in surgery. They're getting the bullet out of his leg."

The air rushed out of Toshiro as though Pierce had kicked him in the stomach. Dom got an arm around his waist to help him into a chair before he collapsed. He heard none of her whispered assurances; he felt as though his head had been shoved into a wind tunnel.

Dropping his head down between his knees, Toshiro tried to keep himself conscious. The doctor rushed over to check on him. He waved her off.

"He's going to be fine?"

"Perfectly fine. You can see him in a few hours," the doctor promised him. "Now, as I've finished checking on Pierce, I'll leave you three to catch up while I make my rounds."

"Dom? Do me a favour, give Charlie and Jude a call to let them know it's all okay?" Toshiro nodded towards the door. He wanted a moment to talk to Pierce alone. "Please?"

With Dom out of the room, Toshiro switched from the chair by the door to the one beside the bed. He pressed Pierce to give him the full details of what happened, though there wasn't much to say. It didn't matter to him; he held on illogically to the idea that being told everything would settle his panic about his husband's injuries.

"Toshiro." Pierce tried to reach out to him, but his injuries kept him on the bed. "You've heard the basics. Details won't change any of it. Mack will come out of this with likely nothing more than a new scar."

"Will he be arrested for Rafe's death?"

Pierce shook his head immediately in answer. "Not a chance. It's a clear case of self-defence. They're hardly likely to find issue with my version of events."

"Where the hell was your protective detail in all of this?" Toshiro wanted someone alive to vent his rage against. Rafe had already met judgement for his actions. "Weren't they supposed to prevent this shit?"

"Someone started a ruckus in the back of the building. They assumed it was Rafe, and left to handle it. It allowed him time to sneak inside." Pierce glared warningly at Toshiro. "They'll be reprimanded for not leaving someone on their post. Rookie mistake. I'd recommend you not go unleash your anger on them. They're still uniformed officers who won't take kindly to being shouted at by you."

"I don't take kindly to my husband being shot while they fuck off. One of them should've stayed behind." Toshiro couldn't believe such a classic rookie mistake had been made. "*Honestly.*"

As it wasn't fair to take his frustration out on an injured man, Toshiro let it go for the moment. He left the room once Dom returned to pace the hall. His nerves wouldn't settle until he could see Mack with his own eyes.

Toshiro (and the nurses) eventually tired of his pacing. He dropped into one of the rows of seats along the wall. His foot tapped incessantly on the floor in time with his fingers against his leg.

What's taking them so long?

It's just a bullet.

In Mack's leg.

Oh God.

"Tosh?" Dom crouched in front of him, snapping her fingers in front of his face. "You can see him now. They've put him in the room next to Pierce's. The doctor—"

Not waiting to hear the rest, Toshiro shoved Dom out of the way and raced down the hall. He skidded across the slick floor, coming to a halt in front of the door. A uniformed officer opened it for him before closing it after he'd stepped inside.

Perching on the edge of the hospital bed, Toshiro lifted one of his husband's limp hands into his own. He carefully clutched at the lifeless fingers. For a man who spoke so many languages, words failed him for once.

"Think we're getting too old for this shit." Mack's groggily spoken joke broke the stark silence of the room. "Are you actually crying? Tosh. *Love.* Come here."

Careful of the wires, Toshiro shifted up onto the mattress beside his husband. They clung to each other. He wondered if the universe hadn't been sending them a sign to make a few changes in their lives with so many close calls.

"What're you thinking about?" Mack asked.

"Retiring. Maybe we should actually be what our covers are for a while." Toshiro brought gentle hands up to frame Mack's face, bringing him closer for an unhurried, hungry kiss. "No heists. No risks. No almost dying."

"No more heists?" Mack brushed his lips against Toshiro's several times. "Can we actually manage it?"

"I love you enough to try."

EPILOGUE

MACK
SEVERAL MONTHS LATER.

The trip to Ishinomaki in the Miyagi Prefecture had seemed to take forever. Sixteen hours on a plane followed by three hours on a train. Mack thought his arse would have blistered by the time they finally arrived at the little inn they'd rented out for two weeks.

Their trip had been delayed by a few days, but they managed to arrive in time to complete what his mother-in-law called *higan*. A tradition that if Mack understood correctly involved spending seven days paying respect to one's ancestors. They all went to support her visit the place where her family had once lived.

None of the houses in her childhood neighbourhood had been left standing. The tsunami had washed all of them away. The debris-filled water had claimed the lives of three thousand people, which included all of the Uedas who called Ishinomaki home.

On their first morning in the city, they woke before dawn

to drive up to the stone memorial constructed in memory of the tsunami victims. His mother-in-law knelt before the fan-shape monument. Her tears flowed steadily as her children joined her.

The older woman reached back to grip the hands of her twins. She'd leaned heavily on them for the trip thus far, for once allowing her twins to be her strength. Mack had always admired the might of the tiny Ueda matriarch.

Mack stayed back to allow them to mourn. He glanced over at Dom to find her also hovering awkwardly off to the side. None of them aside from his mother-in-law were religious by any stretch of the imagination.

As she offered her prayers, Mack found his attention straying to the last few months. They'd buried Rafe, seen Trev and Mary sent to prison, and Pierce found enough evidence to bring several others to justice, including the arms dealer. Their group had breathed massive sighs of relief with the threat wholly removed from their lives.

Given Rafe's admission of guilt, Mack had assumed his father would immediately be released from prison. He wasn't. Pierce fought hard to enter his own testimony, but no one wanted to listen.

They continued to fight. Mack only hoped they found success before his father died. His health deteriorated at a terrifying speed.

The fear of losing his father had almost kept him from the trip. Mack didn't like the idea of being so far away from home if the worst happened. In the end, Toshiro leaving for two weeks without him had been too unbearable to imagine.

They'd almost lost each other so many times. Mack hadn't found the strength to watch him jet off to Japan alone. Toshiro had felt the same way; they'd struggled in the aftermath of the shooting.

Nightmares. Separation anxiety.

His uncle called it post-traumatic stress. Mack thought he just needed time. The memories would fade; one day he'd forget Rafe's name and the harm the man had caused his family.

I'll never forgive the bastard for trying to kill Tosh.

The shooting wasn't what kept Mack up at night. His nightmares revolved around the brief period when he'd believe Toshiro was dead. He constantly dreamt about finding his husband's body.

Maybe I will give the therapist Pierce recommended a call.

Talking can't hurt anything, can it?

The other significant change in their lives had been the lack of heists. *Greatest, and most boring difference.* Mack hated it. He'd quickly grown tired of actually being a philanthropist; it lacked the excitement that came from planning a job.

He wasn't the only one. A few months into their promise to leave thieving behind them, the entire group itched for something more exciting. Dom and Charlie had tried everything from hiking to hang gliding. Jude had picked up wheelchair ultimate Frisbee, or Whisbee.

None of it worked.

Bored thieves were dangerous ones.

Something has to give.

"Mack?" Dom inched over to him. She handed over her mobile that had a news article pulled up. "Have a read."

The article detailed the recent theft of several centuries-old carvings. A gang had taken them in a blatant heist in the middle of the day from the home of a man in his eighties. They'd been passed down from generation to generation in his family.

Bastards.

We should get them back for him.

"We're retired," Mack whispered to Dom. He grinned apologetically to Toshiro, who glared at him over his shoulder.

"But *Mack*," she whined.

"Shh. Praying is happening." Mack nudged her with his arm.

A sharp wave from his mother-in-law had both Mack and Dom stepping up beside their significant others. After learning of their near-death experiences, Mrs Ueda had made an even more concerted effort to treat her son- and daughter-in-law as family. She'd embraced them completely.

After the memorial, the group travelled across the city to drive through the streets Toshiro's mum remembered. Her family home hadn't been rebuilt. She placed several *ohagi* by the foundation, offering further prayers.

Over a quiet tea ceremony, his mother-in-law told them stories from her childhood. She seemed lighter for having paid her respects. More open. Her tales strayed to the happier times, lifting all of their spirits.

They'd visit the cemetery the next day. Toshiro had told him about the red bean paste-covered sweet rice that would be left at each tomb, along with incense. His husband might not be religious, but he respected his family heritage.

Later that evening, they stood by a railing looking out across the Ishinomaki Bay. Dom and Charlie had gone off with his mother-in-law for supper to allow the two men some time alone. They'd return the favour eventually.

"Are you bored?" Mack moved behind Toshiro, arms wrapped around him with his chin resting on his husband's shoulder. "Not with me, mind you, but with life."

"A bit," Toshiro admitted after a minute of thought. He twisted his head slightly to glance at Mack's face. "What've you got in mind, Gregor?"

Showing Toshiro the article, Mack pondered the pros and cons. They'd only been out of the business for a few months. Maybe it was better to give themselves more time to adjust to a normal sort of life.

Or we'll die of boredom.

"Tosh?" Mack shifted slightly to nibble at his husband's ear. "What do you think?"

"One last heist?"

"One last heist." Mack had a distinct feeling it might be more than one. "Have I mentioned I fucking love you?"

"Ich liebe dich in allen sprachen in der welt."

"Gesundheit." Mack squeezed his arms around Toshiro. "What does that mean?"

"I love you in all the languages of the world." His husband smiled brilliantly at him. "Maybe two more heists? Just to be sure."

"Brilliant."

THE END

ACKNOWLEDGEMENTS

A massive thank you to my brilliant betas who take my first draft and help me turn it into something legible. To Becky, Olivia, and all the fantastic people at Hot Tree. And also, to my beloved hubby who answered a tonne of questions about locks (handy being married to a master locksmith) and to Bacon for keeping me company while I write (my dog, not the food--actually, thanks to crispy bacon as well.)

And, lastly, thank you, readers, for following me on my writing journey. I hope you enjoyed the Mack & Toshi ride.

ABOUT THE AUTHOR

Dahlia Donovan wrote her first romance series after a crazy dream about shifters and damsels in distress. She prefers irreverent humour and unconventional characters.

An autistic and occasional hermit, her life wouldn't be complete without her husband and her massive collection of books and video games.

Stay connected with Dahlia:

FACEBOOK: WWW.FACEBOOK.COM/DAHLIADONOVAN

WEBSITE: WWW.DAHLIADONOVAN.COM

TWITTER: WWW.TWITTER.COM/DAHLIADONOVAN

ABOUT THE PUBLISHER

Hot Tree Publishing opened its doors in 2015 with an aspiration to bring quality fiction to the world of readers. With the initial focus on romance and a wide spread of romance sub-genres, we envision opening up to alternative genres in the near future.

Firmly seated in the industry as a leading editing provider to independent authors and small publishing houses, Hot Tree Publishing is the sister company to Hot Tree Editing, founded in 2012. Having established in-house editing and promotions, plus having a well-respected market presence, Hot Tree Publishing endeavors to be a leader in bringing quality stories to the world of readers.

Interested in discovering more amazing reads brought to you by Hot Tree Publishing? Head over to the website for information:

WWW.HOTTREEPUBLISHING.COM